T. M. DELANEY

Eerie

A Collection of 10 Chilling Tales

Copyright © 2020 by T. M. Delaney

All rights reserved. No part of this publication may be reproduced, stored or transmitted in any form or by any means, electronic, mechanical, photocopying, recording, scanning, or otherwise without written permission from the publisher. It is illegal to copy this book, post it to a website, or distribute it by any other means without permission.

This novel is entirely a work of fiction. The names, characters and incidents portrayed in it are the work of the author's imagination. Any resemblance to actual persons, living or dead, events or localities is entirely coincidental.

T. M. Delaney asserts the moral right to be identified as the author of this work.

T. M. Delaney has no responsibility for the persistence or accuracy of URLs for external or third-party Internet Websites referred to in this publication and does not guarantee that any content on such Websites is, or will remain, accurate or appropriate.

Designations used by companies to distinguish their products are often claimed as trademarks. All brand names and product names used in this book and on its cover are trade names, service marks, trademarks and registered trademarks of their respective owners. The publishers and the book are not associated with any product or vendor mentioned in this book. None of the companies referenced within the book have endorsed the book.

Cover photo by Annie Spratt on Unsplash
Cover font from sinisterfonts.com

First edition

This book was professionally typeset on Reedsy.
Find out more at reedsy.com

*To everyone who loves a good scare.
Thank you for reading my book.*

Contents

Watcher	1
Guilt	6
The Sheep	14
Reflection	23
Punchinello	30
Evil is as Evil Does	40
Invitation	50
Daughter Dearest	60
Infection	68
Unkempt Hair	78
About the Author	99
Also by T. M. Delaney	101

Watcher

A person ought to be able to expect a modicum of privacy in their own home. Especially someone like me, who lives on a corner lot in a small rural neighborhood where the houses are more than a few inches apart from each other. I should be free from all prying eyes. But I'm not. The people across the street, they act so innocent, just the perfect little nuclear family, but they're always watching me. Always *spying* on me, and I don't appreciate it one bit.

It started off innocently enough. I moved into my house after they already lived in theirs. As all my things were brought in, I saw them out in their yard watching, all cheery smiles. They had it all set up to look normal: a child's plastic pool filled with water and screaming kids, the two parents and a grandmother sitting nearby chatting and minding the children. But every time I looked at them, they were looking at me, those fake smiles on their faces. Unnerved, I waved at them, hoping that would stop the stares. Maybe that day it did, because shortly after, they moved their gathering to the backyard; I had to lean out of my bedroom window to be sure, but I confirmed that's where they had moved.

But they just proved bolder the very next day, eyeing me and my house every time they stepped out of their house. Walking to the mailbox? Looking at me. Backing out the car? Looking at me. Digging in the flower bed? Looking at me. When I'd catch them looking, they would smile and wave, trying to make me think *I* was the one with a problem, but I wasn't the one spying on my neighbors, now was I?

As the year dragged on, they got sneakier about their spying. No longer did they linger on the doorstep to say goodbye, obviously casting their gazes over to my home. No longer did they use an excessive amount of caution and slow speed while backing out of their driveway. But even still, I was vigilant, and I caught on to their subterfuge. Oh yes, they were still watching me.

They had gauzy curtains over their windows, but no blinds; they didn't want to cover their view of me, you see. I knew they were watching through those blinds. Even got binoculars one day at the store to confirm my beliefs. The first window I tried opened into the living room, and at the back of the room, in an armchair, sat the man, staring straight back at me. I nearly dropped my binoculars in my fright. Why did they do this? Why were they always, always *watching?*

I tried calling the police to file a complaint, but it did no good. The fool on the other end of the phone sounded confused. As if understanding that one's neighbors are sneaking, spying stalkers is that difficult. I tried to explain the proof I'd obtained with my binoculars, but that only confused the idiot further until finally I just hung up. I was on my own. Me versus them. Well I had bought a lovely home. I wasn't about to give it up because they were watching. I would outlast their invasive eyes.

A year turned into two, and their methods became even subtler still. Now the gauzy curtains were buffeted by blinds. Now they no longer used the front door, relying solely on the back door that opened into the fenced backyard, which could only be exited by a gate in the far side of the fence. I learned their new layout while making a pass around the house in the dark of night. I didn't know what they wanted. I couldn't risk confrontation, but I had to know how they were still doing it, why I could still *feel* those eyes on me at all times.

They must have had disagreements about their methods, because I heard raised voices coming from their home more frequently than ever before. Good, I thought. They were wearing down while I was still yet strong. Eventually, I saw them so infrequently that I began to wonder at my own surety that they were still watching. My gut said they were, but I had to know for sure. To prove it to myself, I crept across the street one evening and pressed myself up against the windows, peering through the slits between the blinds. And sure as anything, there they were, all in the room together, all looking right at me! I jumped and ran pell-mell for my home, certain that at any moment I would feel hands close around my limbs and bring me to the ground.

I made it to my home and flung the door open, only pausing for a moment to look back once I was safely past the threshold. Across the street, light spilled out across their front lawn from the open front door. The man and the woman stood there together, brazenly watching me from right out in the open! There was a look of such rage on their faces, I was sure that I was done for. Quickly, I snapped my door closed and locked it.

For days I was sure the end would be near. I kept my own blinds shut tight, scarce confident enough to peer through them regularly to keep an eye on the watchers. There seemed to be a lot more activity over there. I began to wonder if they were plotting something even more sinister than their spying.

Calling in reinforcements, maybe?

And then the police cars stopped by. For a brief moment, I had hope that my call had done some good and help had finally arrived. But my call had been made months prior, and before long I had proof that help wasn't coming for me. The police must be in on it too. That would explain the fool I'd spoken to so long ago. The police stood on the doorstep for quite a while, speaking with the man and woman of the home, all of them frequently flitting their eyes over at me. I could feel the terror take, wondering if I'd misjudged the entire situation, that I wasn't really strong enough to hold my ground and keep my home.

Then the police made their way across the street for me. I fled from the door and hid under my bed. Several times I heard the pounding of their fists on my door and muffled words from their mouths, but I stayed put. I wouldn't give them any opportunity to hurt me. Finally, the sound ceased, and I slowly crept back out to see what was going on. Now, only the man was outside speaking with the cops. His voice was loud, though the words indistinct, and he gesticulated wildly with his speech, pointing and looking frequently at me. The cops only shook their heads, though, and they turned to leave.

After they drove away, the man still stayed out there, eyes on my home. I felt emboldened now. The police weren't complete fools after all; they *knew* he was the culprit, not me. Maybe they weren't going to arrest him, but they were leaving me alone. I raised my blinds so that he could see that I saw him and that I was unafraid. I smirked and even laughed, thrilled at the power I now felt in the face of their failure. He grit his teeth and started to cross his lawn, and I would have met him at my door had he continued, but his wife appeared at their door, child in arms, and called him back. He turned his rage on her then instead of me, and they withdrew back inside again. Inside, but still watching. But I didn't fuss about is as much now. My gut told me I'd won.

Maybe a week later, a moving truck appeared in front of the house. All of their belongings poured forth from the home and into the truck, the moving men making short work of the contents. All the while, the family watched me. Even some of the moving men watched too, taking cues from their employers. But I had every blind open. Let them watch. I had won. Let them see my victory! Let them see that it was *I* who outlasted them, *I* who didn't break under their constant scrutiny. Let *them* now know how it feels to be under the watchful eye of a stranger at all times. I stood there beside my front window, unmoving, for hours until their home was empty and they themselves had driven off into the night for the final time. I enjoyed the sleep of the just that night, finally free of their abuse.

It didn't take long for a new family to buy the vacated home, the housing market being what it was. When I heard their moving truck arrive, I jumped to! This time, my position would be made clear from the start. I was no victim. I stood out on my porch, hands on hips, feet in a wide, strong stance, and I watched them as they moved in. They gave a few surreptitious glances and a cautious wave at one point. I waved in returned and smiled broadly. I could tell immediately that they were snoops, but it was also evident that they were put off by my confidence. With any luck, this would turn their gazes to a different neighbor.

But if not, I would be fine. I had withstood worse and was all the stronger for it. I knew this game well, and if they insisted, I would play it—and win—again.

Guilt

When I wake up, I have no idea where I am or what is going on. First, I become aware of strange beeps and other sounds. The air is permeated by a strange, almost noxious smell. Faint voices are talking not too far from me. I open my eyes, but the room is so bright, I have to close them again, tears stinging my eyes. I try to speak and ask the voices what's happening, but my mouth won't cooperate. My vocal cords apparently do their part, because a garbled sound manages to make its way out. The two voices briefly fall silent, and then everything whisks into motion.

"I need Dr. Callahan in here right away, please," says a calm voice.

"Oh my gosh, honey!" says another much louder voice. At the same time, a hand touches my face, almost making me wince. Going from nothing to so much stimulation so fast is overwhelming. Through the shock, I vaguely recognize the voice as belonging to my mother. "Honey, you're awake! How are you feeling?"

"Ma'am, please step back. We need to examine her and take her vitals." More hands touch my hands and wrist. "Miss, can you tell me your name?"

Woozily, I shake my head. It's all too much. Still, somehow I manage to rally myself and say, "Anna." A chorus of positivity tells me they're pleased with the answer, but I let myself slip away a little. It's too much all at once. I'm not ready. Vaguely, I know something must be wrong for me to be in a hospital. Hospital. Somehow, unbidden, the word comes to me. What happened to me?

~~~

I spend an interminable amount of time in the hospital. Consciousness comes and goes. People come and go. Tons of people. Some I know, some I don't. Some who talk to me, some who don't, some who yell, some who comfort me. Some in hospital garb, some not. Finally as the time passes, I get my answer.

A train accident they say. A catastrophic one that killed all 156 people on the train. Except for one. Just hearing that feels weird. Somehow wrong. I can't wrap my head around it. Not around how many people had been wiped off the earth in one fell swoop, not that I'd had such a close brush with death, not that I'd somehow been the "lucky" one.

Lucky. That's all everyone wants to say to me, some warmly, some snidely. The doctors, the nurses, my mother, and all the others. "You're one lucky girl!" "It's so lucky that you made it out alive!" "A mild head injury and nothing else; so lucky!" "Hmph. Must be nice to be so lucky." It doesn't feel lucky. It feels cruel…wrong. Why should I have made it when all those others didn't? Was it just some kind of—

~~~

"Survivor's guilt," the therapist says. "It's quite common after experiencing a trauma such as the one you have."

I eyeball the therapist bemusedly. Her words aren't a surprise at all. "Yeah," I reply, "I gathered all of that. What do I do about it?" I scrutinize the other person in the room, uncomfortable with his presence. I have no way to communicate that to the therapist, though.

"There are several things you can do," the therapist begins. "First and foremost, you have to take care of yourself. I can see from looking at you that you aren't getting enough sleep. If you are struggling with that, you should consider taking a nonaddictive sleep aid for a while."

Of course I can't sleep much. They won't let me. Taking a sleeping pill might work, but the idea of being solidly unconscious in their presence concerns me. "Yeah, I'll do what I can," I say dismissively. "What else?"

She raises an eyebrow slightly, but says nothing, only pausing to jot down a note on her notepad. "It also helps to stop and consider everything logically. You were not responsible for the accident, so you cannot apply blame to yourself for surviving. Also, realize that luck is random; you can 'steal' it from someone else. And finally, try to focus on how your survival impacts your loved ones. Think of how happy your mother is that you're still alive."

I think back to how tightly my mother hugged me this morning and every morning since I left the hospital. And yet I can't help but wonder, if she knew everything, if she saw what I see and felt what I feel, would she still feel the same way? Would she still want me around? Would she feel okay if she were me? I can't say for certain. All I know for sure is that I am alone. At least, in a manner of speaking. I give a sidelong glance at the man across the room again.

"Oh, you can also try doing something meaningful for others. Sometimes doing good for the world can help reduce the feeling that you don't deserve to be here."

In my peripheral vision, I see the man smile. I know one thing I could do that would make many people happy, but I'm not willing to. The price is too steep. All the same, I nod my head. "Thank you for the advice," I say, reaching out my hand to shake hers as I stand to leave. "It's very helpful." It's not, but then again, she doesn't have the full story. Guess that's my fault too. As I rise, so too does the man.

"I'll see you next week?" she asks, eyes searching my face.

I keep it neutral. "Yeah, sounds good." Probably not. Next week is so far away; I feel like I can't be sure of anything. I walk out the front door of her home office, not holding the door for the man who follows. It doesn't matter, though, because he's right on my heels as I pass the threshold.

"You don't seem to feel any better, huh?" he sneers. "Therapy not all you hoped it would be?"

I ignore him and turn to walk down the sidewalk, my pace brisk. I want to get back to my mom's house as soon as possible. Since leaving the hospital, I've been staying with her. A "transitionary period," she calls it. It was her idea initially, but I've since agreed with it wholeheartedly. I do not relish the idea of having to live alone again.

"You'll get yours in the end!" the man hollers as he finally stops following me. "We'll see to it!"

I sigh in relief as I get farther and farther away from him, but all the same, I keep my eyes peeled. He's annoying for sure, but he's also not the worst. I find myself wondering if I should have been more forthright with my therapist. But how can I do that? How does one explain what I'm experiencing without being locked in the nut house? *Gee, doc, this whole "letting go of guilt" thing isn't really working for me. You see, the dead keep coming to tell me how pissed off they are.*

Right on cue, a girl who is much younger than I am with a face twisted in spiteful glee fades into view and takes step beside me. "He's really angry, you know."

"Who? Frank?" I mutter, referring to the man who'd just helped himself to a seat at my therapy session.

"No," she snipes, smacking gum as she talks. I wonder at that. She isn't corporeal, so how does she have gum? Did she die with gum in her mouth? Is she fated to chew gum for the rest of eternity? I'd probably hate everything too if that happened to me. *"He* is," she says, pointing.

I look up and stop dead in my tracks. Before me stands an honest-to-goodness grim reaper. No, not stands. *Floats.* Black hooded robe, endless void in place of a face. Scythe. The works. "What the...." I can't summon any other words, the sight of him somehow far more shocking than seeing the vengeful spirits of all those dead passengers from the train wreck.

"That's Death!" the girl chirps gleefully. "And he is *furious* that you escaped. So now, he's coming after you!" She giggles and spins in front of me, a macabre spectacle of the joyful youth she must have been in life. "You're already his," she adds. "You just don't know it."

Finally, my shock wears away, leaving stubborn anger in its place. "We all have to die someday," I say, staring into the void under his hood. "But doesn't mean it has to be anytime soon. It's not *my* fault if you screwed up that day. I don't owe you anything. So suck it." As I pivot on my heel and march away, I felt sick to my stomach. I just mouthed off to Death, but instead of feeling satisfaction, I feel fear. What kind of idiot challenges

Death to his own game?

~~~

A few days go by business as usual; I don't even see any of the spirits from the train accident. I try to keep my guard up because I know it can't possibly be over this easily, but slowly I relax and begin to wonder if maybe everything will be fine after all. Just long enough for a sense of security to set in before everything ramps up 1,000-fold.

Next thing I know, everywhere I go, everywhere I look, the train accident victims are present. In my room watching me sleep and shouting and causing a ruckus every couple of hours to be sure I don't get any rest. In my bathroom, leering as I tried to shower and get ready for the day. All along the sidewalk as I walk to the bus stop to head to work. On the bus itself, phasing through the living passengers on the crowded bus. My cubicle at work is packed full of them, and they hum under their breath all day so that I can never quite maintain concentration. At the coffee shop after work where the cute barista flirts with me, they sneer and make kissy faces, ruining any chance I have of pursuing a relationship.

On and on this torment goes. Even worse than their constant presence and annoying noise is the feeling of intense rage and frustration that I can feel oozing off of all of them. It's sticky and vile like polluted, oily water that washes over me and sticks and can't be wiped away. They are *angry* that I lived when they didn't, that I have a chance to continue my life when they do not.

Somewhere in the back of my frazzled mind, I understand that it must be worse because I'm the only one who made it rather than one of several survivors. I don't want to understand it, and I don't want to feel sympathy for them. I don't want to feel like they're right, but it's so hard under that constant onslaught. I try to remember the things the therapist told me, but it's all so hard to focus on. I wish more than anything I could talk to someone about this, but this just isn't *normal.* People don't see these kinds of things. You can't just fall apart because something bad happened to you. I look in the mirror and see my red-rimmed eyes and my pale, gaunt face, and I know how much of a disappointment I must be to people like my mother who want to see me be successful. I must keep up the facade. I must!

It goes on for weeks and weeks. I do everything I can to put them out of my mind, watching TV, reading books, visiting friends, meditating, praying. I keep up the outward facade, but it doesn't change anything inside me. And it doesn't change the situation; every moment, they remain, always there, always reminding me how I have no right to be here, no right to be happy.

And eventually, I realize I don't have a choice anymore. It comes out of the blue, as I'm walking from the office to the bus stop, on my way from the bustling city back to my suburban home. I come to understand that I *had* been wrong before. I *do* owe Death, and not only that, I owe *all* those people that had been on that final journey together. So I deviate from the path down an alley alongside a skyscraper. As though it's there just for me, I find a fire escape leading all the way to the roof. Calmly, I climb it, step after step until I make it to the roof.

I cross the roof and stand on the ledge and contemplate the distance. It looks both far and close. I wonder if I'll feel anything; I wonder if the passengers from the train felt anything.

Remembering them, I turn around and find all of them behind me. It seems all 156 have shown up for this moment to witness what they've been working so hard to accomplish. I see their eagerness, and through the fog in my head it sickens me. A voice in my head questions if this really is the way, but it's so very far away. "You're all getting what you want," I say. "I hope this brings you some peace."

Then I look at the back of the crowd and see him. Death. Just a floating, solemn presence, and though he has no face, it's like I can see smug satisfaction in his countenance. I haven't seen him since the day I left the therapist's office, and now instead of fear, I feel indignation. What am I doing? How has it come to this? "No!" I whisper. "Screw you all!" I scream. But as I try to step away, suddenly with an unearthly roar, all of the spirits rush at me. Though incorporeal, the force of them rocks me off balance, and my eyes open wide as I feel myself topple over the edge.

Everything moves into slow motion. All around me are the twisted faces of what's left of the other passengers' souls. I turn my head and see the ground moving for me. There, beside the place I will land, Death waits calmly for the prize he is due. And the last thing I know is this: *I don't want to die.*

The Sheep

Jerry sighed and dropped his head to his chest, hands gripping his steering wheel. New house in the boonies, new job that was his "only chance to not become a worthless layabout" (to use his mother's words), and a six-a.m. departure time. Could his life get any worse? With a groan, he started the car and backed out of the driveway before his mom could come running out to yell at him some more. She was still super angry with him for getting expelled from school.

He shrugged his shoulders dismissively as he began driving. He still didn't really see what the big deal was. His grades were already pretty terrible to begin with, so it wasn't like he was getting much out of being there. And the expulsion was completely unfair: so what he'd brought a gun to school to loan to a friend? He was hardly the only person to ever bring a gun to school, and his buddy Chris had said he needed it, and when Chris asked for something, you did it. He was the leader of their crew. But now that he wasn't allowed back at school, Chris had apparently written him off since he'd gotten caught and hadn't been in contact since. Jerry seethed, angry at the unfair turn of events he'd been oppressed with.

And worst of all, Jerry's mom had taken his gun away, which was bullshit in his opinion since he'd paid for that gun with his own money. His dad had been right when he'd said to keep the gun secret from his mom. But at least he was only a few months away from turning eighteen. Once he was legally an adult, he could demand his gun back, and he could move out to somewhere better than the middle of nowhere hovel that his mom had forced him to join her in when custody was taken away from his dad during the whole gun fiasco. He'd also be able to get a better job than working at some kind of tree nursery.

He drew himself from his thoughts just in time to realize he was about to miss his turn onto a road so surrounded by bushes and trees it was nearly swallowed from view. He cursed and instinctively slammed on the brakes, swerving into the turn. Belatedly, he realized he should have checked the rear view first to be sure no one was behind him, but again, he just shrugged his shoulders. The person who did the rear ending was always at fault, so it wouldn't have mattered. Probably could've even got a few days off of work over it.

He drove along the narrow country road a short way and came to a one-way bridge at a strange, cock-eyed angle. A glance ahead confirmed that no one else was coming, so he maneuvered his car up onto the bridge and crossed it. Just on the other side of the bridge, in his peripheral vision, he noticed something white off to his left. He turned his head to try and look at it, but he was already past it. White rocks maybe? But it had seemed almost uniform, like a ring or something. Not likely to be natural. He shrugged and told himself to look for it on the way back, curious what it had been.

He got to the nursery and met his boss who he could tell, just from the first words he said, was going to be a huge pain to deal with. Then he started learning about how to take care of the plants. His day picked up considerably at his lunch break when he met the other workers and learned that at least a couple of them weren't major flora nerds like the boss. And then finally the day was done and he could head home. As he approached the bridge, he glanced to his right to try and see what he'd seen that morning, but the lighting was already dim and the angle from this direction was worse, so again all he could see was a uniform flash of white. Not knowing what it was bugged him. *Tomorrow morning*, he thought. He'd make sure to see it then.

~~~

After a mostly relaxing night only interrupted by his nagging mom pestering him for details about his first day of work, Jerry was annoyed to once again be awoken by his alarm clock to face another day. He followed the same route as before, this time successfully remembering his turn off of the county road before he was nearly past it. He was crossing over the bridge, though, before he remembered he'd wanted to see what was in that small clearing. He slowed down as he crossed the bridge and looked to his left. And this time, he saw it. It wasn't a ring of rocks; it was a ring of wooden sheep statues.

He looked around as he continued on, and he was surprised to see that there wasn't a house nearby. Whose property was it, then? And why on earth would they set up a bunch of sheep statues in an oblong circle? He shrugged his shoulders and carried on with his commute, but he couldn't quite put the sheep out of his mind.

At work, he went through the motions, putting forth the least effort possible to complete each task. Hey, it wasn't like *he* had any passion for the plants, he figured. He was just there for the money. At lunch, he asked his two new buddies if they'd ever seen the sheep statues, still unable to quell the curiosity bubbling inside him. Both of them said "no" and gave him strange looks, so he quickly shut up about the topic, not wanting to ostracize himself from the only good aspect of the job.

After work, he headed home once again. And once again, as he approached that bridge, he turned to look at the clearing. Now that he knew what he was looking for, he was able to spot it, even in the dim lighting. Why sheep? he wondered. Why all gathered in a circle? He couldn't shake the thought from his mind. That night, he tried asking his mom about it, but she wasn't cooperative, unwilling to let him switch the topic to something trivial, in her opinion, instead of grilling him about his new job. He finally gave up on her and went to his room. She wasn't going to be any help.

~~~

Each day that dawned that week, he thought of the sheep as he approached their location, looking over at them each time he passed. Why were they there? It was so weird! It drove him even more crazy that he couldn't talk to anyone about them. The guys at work would think he was nuts, and his mom would probably find some reason to nag at him about them. He was cut off from all his old school friends now too, and even they probably wouldn't have understood his obsession. Heck, even *he* didn't understand it!

On Saturday, he had to go to work for a short afternoon shift, and he found himself idling in his car in the middle of the road, staring at the sheep on his way to his job. He felt attracted to them, as though they were pulling at him, calling to him. As he observed them, his vision almost seemed to tunnel in on them, blocking everything else from his view until there was nothing but sheep. Maybe he would get out of the car and take a closer look....

As he started to reach for the door, a loud honk behind him snapped him from his trance. He looked up in his rear view mirror to see a man in a truck stuck behind him on the one-way bridge, angrily gesticulating at him. He raised his hand to flip the man the bird before pulling forward, and he maintained a purposely slow pace solely to antagonize the man for honking at him. He smirked as the man finally whipped his truck around him and peeled off into the distance. *What a jerk*, he thought.

At work, he overheard the other guys talking about some kind of deal going down that evening. It sounded like they planned on picking up some drugs at a party that they could then go out and sell. When they saw him listening in, they asked if he wanted in on the action. He knew that he really should avoid getting into any more trouble right away since the gun thing had just happened, but he also knew that if he said no, the guys would probably just think he was a wuss and not talk to him anymore. And besides, it wasn't like he was guaranteed to get caught if he sold a few drugs on the side. So he quickly told them he was interested, and they pulled him in, giving him the scoop.

After work, he followed behind the guys to head straight for the party, heading a completely different direction from the one he normally took. The party was a blast, and he made eyes at a lot of the girls there while he and his friends waited for their contact to show up. Once the dealer arrived, they each took a cut of the product, each handing over their portion of the cash payment, and then they went their separate ways. Jerry decided to enjoy the party a little before leaving, hooking up with a cute girl who he'd caught staring at him earlier. After a few hours of fun, he headed back for his mom's house, struggling to drive straight since he'd had a few beers. He'd thought about stopping after only two, but everyone else was drinking a bunch, so he kept up with them, not wanting to stand out.

When he reached the turnoff for his work, he slowed down, preparing to turn on it. At the last minute, he remembered the time of day, or rather night, and passed the road by. He shook his head. What on earth would compel him to head for work in the middle of the night? When he made it home, he blew off him mom and her screams about him smelling like booze, just pushing his way to his bedroom, locking the door, and collapsing on the bed to get some much-needed rest. But he struggled to fall asleep, visions of sheep literally jumping through his mind's eye. Wasn't counting sheep supposed to *help* people fall asleep? After what felt like an eternity, he finally managed to nod off.

~~~

The next week passed in much the same way as the first: drive to work, slack through work, try to fit in with the guys, drive home, dodge nagging mom. It took no time at all for Jerry to get used to the monotonous rhythm, but all the while, he was plagued with ever-growing thoughts about the sheep statues. Each morning he was almost eager to see them and just as disappointed to pass them by as he drove to work, where he would spend the day half distracted thinking about his drive home when he could see the sheep again. At night, his dreams were plagued with images of sheep that seemed to call to him. He wanted so badly to respond, and sometimes would wake in the night and have to resist the itching urge to go out and see the sheep statues. Through it all, a small voice in the back of his head warned him that something was wrong, but he didn't listen to it much; he didn't want to.

Finally, on Sunday morning the conflicting thoughts for and against the sheep rose to a crescendo in his mind, and his resolve to not say anything to his mother crumbled. He casually mentioned that he'd spotted something interesting along the drive he took to work and asked her if she'd come look at it with him. She looked at him oddly, but agreed, much to his relief. He wanted to see someone else's reaction to the sheep.

They got in the car, and he drove her over to the sheep. When they arrived, he pointed to the cluster of sheep, told her how interesting he thought they were, and asked her what she thought. When she asked if he was serious, he got angry and screamed at her to look at them. After sparing him another odd look, she obliged him and studied the sheep. He watched in eager anticipation, waiting for her to say she felt the same. Finally, she shrugged her shoulder and told him that they creeped her out, like there was something wrong with them. Then she pointed and added to her judgment that she really didn't like the look of the coyote statue lurking in the background.

Puzzled, Jerry looked back at the little clearing, and he realized that she was right. In the shadows just behind the sheep was a gnarled, haggard looking wooden statue of a coyote. He sat frozen in his seat, staring into the eyes of the coyote, which almost seemed to hold a smug malevolence. He jumped as his mom barked at him to drive her home. Annoyed that she hadn't had the same reaction as he did and that he felt more confused than ever, he grumbled and maneuvered a three-point turn in the road to take them back home.

~~~

Later that night, he sat thinking of the sheep again. Already, the memory of the coyote had faded; it hadn't really been as eerie as he previously thought, surely. It was the sheep that were compelling. And suddenly, he knew he wanted to actually get out of his car and walk over to them. He wanted to touch them. Maybe even sit by them. If only he could just be among them, that would make him feel so good.

And so it was that he found himself sneaking out of the house in the darkest hour of night, slipping into his car, and pulling out of the gravel driveway as quietly as he could to avoid waking his mother. Luckily for him, she'd always been a heavy sleeper. In no time, he'd reached the one-lane bridge. He pulled off the road just before the bridge, not wanting some crazy yahoo to come speeding by and run into his truck on the other side. Then he climbed out and marched purposely across the bridge, lighting the way with a flashlight he'd grabbed from one of the drawers in the kitchen.

And then he was there, standing at the side of the road looking upon the group of sheep. He felt such a feeling of longing in his chest that it nearly ached. He walked forward, and then he was among them. He reached out his hand, trailing it along first one and then another, loving the tactile sensation of their presence. Finally, he sat down in the grass, and at that moment, everything changed. The flashlight fell from his hand as his body convulsed, filling him with pain. He found himself frozen, unable to move anything but his eyes. And he felt thin and hollow, almost as though he were nothing more than a shell of wood. He swung his eyes around wildly, following the path of the fallen flashlight beam to see the coyote illuminated, it's shadow terrifyingly large on the trees behind it. Jerry tried to scream, but he could make no sound for he could take no breath. He stood locked in the gaze of the coyote, which seemed to sneer and somehow move closer, and then there was a snarling growl followed by nothing at all.

~~~

Most people didn't pay much mind to the little sheep statues with the coyote lurking ever dangerously, too absorbed in their own individual lives to pay attention to such an odd display. Only one person came by, a woman in search of her wayward son. She stood on the side of the road in the morning, not daring to disobey every instinct that had the hair on the back of her neck standing in alarmed protest. She considered the sheep and coyote before her. Was there another sheep that hadn't been there yesterday? Was there a fresh gleam in the coyote's eye? She couldn't be sure, and in the end, she thought with a sigh, did it really matter anymore? After all, some things just sorted themselves out.

Reflection

Kelly wasn't an overly vain girl. She didn't spend much time paying attention to her reflection. In retrospect, if she had, perhaps her tragic demise could have been avoided. It was eighteen long years before she first noticed anything amiss. She was in her room getting ready for bed, and in her peripheral vision, she thought she saw a flash of movement. Her head snapped up sharply on instinct, but there was nothing there but her own reflection staring back at her with the same startled expression. *Hmm, must've just seen myself move,* she thought to herself. And she went on with her evening without a second thought, not pausing to realize that, when she saw the flash of movement, she herself had been sitting stationary at the foot of the bed, merely flexing her ankles. A long day at the restaurant where she worked had left her achy and tired, so she just climbed into bed and went straight to sleep without any further thought.

Several years went by with the occasional moment such as the one just described, and each time Kelly wrote it off as unimportant. Just her own reflection startling her, or maybe a passing animal if she caught her reflection outside somewhere. Nothing to be concerned about. Nothing to spare any passing thought for. It was another five years after the first occasion, just after Kelly graduated from college and started her very first job at a high-pressure marketing firm, that she really began to take notice that something strange was happening.

As she got ready for work one morning, fussing over her eyeliner that she just could not seem to get even, she thought she saw her reflection's eyes roll. She froze, looking closer. The reflection matched her own scrutiny, *seeming* to do as it was supposed to, but something felt off. The expression in the eyes seemed almost…sinister. Kelly backed away from the mirror uneasily, then closed her eyes and shook her head, dashing from the room as she decided that really, her eyeliner was fine after all. Had she kept her eyes opened, she would have noticed that her reflection did not shake its head.

She went to work as usual, and before long, she forgot about the odd occurrence that morning as she focused on reading emails from clients and colleagues, making a list of the tasks she was responsible for that day and charging forth to do a good job. She worked straight through the morning, not even stopping for a bathroom break until it was time for lunch. One of her new coworkers, a woman named Judy who had been assigned to be her mentor, drew her out of her focused trance.

"Hey, hon, you comin' to lunch?"

Startled, Kelly looked at her watch and blushed. "Gosh, it's already noon?"

Judy chucked. "Darlin', you work too hard. You're young and got a few decades of work ahead of you. Best take it easy before you give yourself a mental breakdown! Now c'mon, let's go."

Kelly smiled. She knew Judy was right that she shouldn't overwork herself. She was just so eager to prove herself and get her career off on the right foot. "Alright, Judy, you're right. Just let me swing by the restroom first."

"I'll come with you," Judy said, rummaging around in her purse. "I need to go too."

The two women walked into the bathroom, chatting away companionably. Judy had her back to the mirror over the vanity and Kelly was facing it. Except her reflection wasn't there. She froze mid-sentence and rubbed at her eyes before looking at the mirror again. Her reflection was there again, staring at her wide-eyed. Judy looked at her quizzically, then over at the mirror. Then she cracked a smile. "You don't look *that* bad, kiddo."

"I...I thought..." Kelly stammered. She didn't know how to say what she'd thought. Judy would think she was nuts. "Guess I'm just tired," she said with a sheepish smile. They both used the bathroom, and Kelly made it out faster, washing her hands as she heard Judy finishing up. She tentatively glanced up at her reflection as she scrubbed her hands. It stared back at her, steady as can be, then winked at her. Kelly stood frozen in shock, and then Judy came out again, resuming their conversation again like nothing had happened. Of course, as far as she was concerned, nothing had. Kelly shot a few nervous glances at her reflection, but it did nothing else untoward before she and Judy exited the bathroom.

For the remainder of the day, Kelly was distracted and unable to focus on her work. She didn't know how to explain what she'd seen. Maybe Judy had been right on-the-nose earlier when she'd joked about her being overworked? That had to be it, right? Reflections couldn't move on their own. All the same, she avoided looking into mirrors for the rest of the day, including once she got home in the evening. If she didn't look, nothing bad could happen. Or so she thought.

The next morning, she woke up determined to forget the

oddities from the previous day. She stared defiantly at her reflection for a few moments, then hopped into the shower, feeling her confidence returning. When she stepped back out of the shower, she scrutinized her reflection again. She smiled lightly, and her reflection complied, but then it grinned toothily. It raised its hand in the air, and as it did, so too did Kelly's hand. "What?" she exclaimed. As she watched, horrified, the reflection's fingers curled into her fist, and against her will, so too did Kelly's. A moment later, their fists swung down in synchrony, punching each full force in their own faces.

Kelly screamed and dropped to the floor, clutching her face and crying. Already her face was swelling, and she knew before long it would begin bruising. She stayed cowered on the floor, terrified to look at the mirror again. What was happening? This couldn't be real! But what was the alternative explanation? That out of the blue she'd just decided to punch herself in the face? Gingerly, she touched her eye and winced as the tender flesh protested the pressure. She would have a black eye, there was no doubt. How on earth would she explain that to her coworkers? How would she explain to them why she shied away from every reflective surface she came across?

She crawled out of the bathroom, resolutely avoiding the mirror, relieved that she no longer had a full-length mirror in her bedroom like she'd had as a child. She got dressed and then grabbed her phone to call work. She was loath to take a sick day so early into her employment, but it was a Friday, and she knew there was no way she would be able to maintain concentration enough for her presence to be effective anyway. After taking appropriate steps to get her sick day, she slipped outside and headed for the park, wanting to get outside and away from mirrors so that she could think.

She spent the entire day wandering outside, circling the park, walking the streets of the old downtown area of the small town she lived in (making sure to keep her eyes averted from the reflective windows of the storefronts) and only speaking to someone once when she stopped to buy lunch at the local deli. The proprietor studied her face with a sympathetic gaze, so she knew the bruising on her face must look horrible. By the end of the day, she'd decided to brush what had happened aside. There was no way to explain what happened and no one who could help her. She would just have to avoid mirrors for a while until whatever was causing her to see and experience impossible things was gone. She couldn't put her whole life on hold for some kind of weird occurrence. *It's just stress,* she thought firmly. Resolved, she finally headed home as the skies were darkening. She headed straight for her bedroom, bypassing the bathroom and its mirror, and went straight to bed.

Some time later, she awoke from a dead sleep with her hackles raised, her body drawing from ingrained instincts to know that something was terribly wrong. She rolled over and looked up to see someone standing over her. She gasped and hurriedly switched on her lamp, only to discover that the person was herself, albeit with a malicious grin spread across her face.

"Hello, other me," the figure said to her. Then it snapped a hand out, grabbing her round the neck and yanking her from her bed.

Kelly gave a strangled scream as she struggled against her foe. But she was too caught off guard by the attack and completely thrown by the appearance of another her, and so was no match for the other who was clearly prepared. As hard as Kelly tried to resist, she found herself being steadily dragged into the bathroom towards the mirror. Everything in her told her that the mirror spelled her doom, so she fought harder, finally managing to break free. She sprinted down the hallway but was tackled from behind.

"Oh no you don't," the other breathed into her ear as she wrapped her fingers tightly into Kelly's hair. "There can't be two of us out here, and I've waited too long for this moment." She pulled hard, drawing a scream of pain from Kelly as she dragged her down the hall again.

Kelly couldn't break the other's grip on her hair, and she couldn't bring herself to struggle hard enough to pull her own hair out. Unable even to form words of protest, she could only sob and stumble as she was dragged along. Finally, they both stood in the bathroom before the mirror, neither casting a reflection in the glass.

The other pulled her close. "I'd say this isn't personal, but I suppose it is since you and I are one and the same. But I will not merely exist anymore. I am going to *live,* and so unfortunately, you are going to have to suffer." Then she shoved Kelly hard towards the mirror.

Kelly winced, expecting to feel a cascade of glass shattering around her, but instead, it seemed to consume her, and she felt herself fall a long way before hitting the floor. She barely had a moment to register what had happened before she found herself moved to her feet with no will of her own, looking at her bathroom mirror. Before her was her reflection. As she watched, the reflection moved, and she moved with it, again, with no will of her own. She watched perplexed as the reflection waved her arms and walked back and forth as she too did the same. Then the reflection leaned against the sink, and so did she, and the reflection winked, and so did she. "All in good order, it looks like," said the reflection, the voice muffled as though spoken through a barrier. Kelly's mouth moved the same way at the same time, but no sound came out.

Growing horror swelled within her, but it did not register on her face, for the reflection felt no horror. And so finally Kelly understood as she turned against her will and walked from the bathroom into a copy of her bedroom, laying down on the bed and closing her eyes though she did not sleep. She wasn't Kelly anymore; she was the reflection.

Punchinello

Myra grit her teeth and clenched her hands on the steering wheel as she eased her jeep through yet another rut in the dirt road she drove along, trying very hard to ignore the incessant chatter of too many voices around her. She cast a sideways glance at her friend Holly, who was sitting backwards on her knees in the passenger seat, talking with the group in the back, most of her attention on Johnny, an attractive boy a couple of years older than them whom she seemed to have a crush on.

This was supposed to have been a road trip for just Myra and Holly, to have some fun before starting their first semesters in college, but right before leaving, Holly had invited a bunch of other people that Myra didn't even know without asking. Not knowing how to say no to the extra people without be labeled a bitch, Myra had gone along with the change in plans. Two days into the trip, though, and she was already regretting it.

"C'mon, babe, pick up the pace!" the boy named Greg moaned from the backseat. "It feels like we've been on this road for ages."

Myra glanced up at the rear view mirror, making eye contact with the complainer. "I never should have let you insist on this 'shortcut,'" she growled in response. "This road is terrible, and I don't even know where we are now." *Or if the quality of this road will continue being passable,* she thought to herself, *or if we'll even make it regardless.* She cast a worried glance at the fuel gauge.

Greg leaned forward, putting his face far too close to hers. "If you're scared, I can take care of the driving for you."

"You're not driving my car," she responded dryly, not bothering to look at him this time.

His girlfriend, Candy, leaned forward, blowing a big bubble of gum as she did. "He'd be getting us wherever the hell we're going a lot faster if he were behind the wheel." Then she grabbed him for a sloppy kiss, saving Myra from figuring out a nice way to point out that a broken axle in the middle of nowhere in the desert in the summer resulting in her death surrounded by a bunch of fools was not the direction she wanted this trip to take.

Myra squinted, trying to see through the haze being raised by the high, blazing sun. "Hey, Holly?" she said, nudging her friend in the side.

Holly turned in her seat and plopped down on Myra's level. "Yeah, what's up?" she asked, her cheery attitude completely at odds with Myra's tired frustration.

Myra pointed. "Does that look like buildings to you?"

Holly shielded her eyes and looked ahead. "Yeah, I think so!" she eventually said. "Do you think we finally found some civilization? I'm starving for dinner." A raucous roar behind her belied everyone else's enthusiasm too.

"Here's hoping it's not a ghost town," Myra muttered to herself as she inched up to the edge of the town. At first, it wasn't promising. The buildings were worn down, and there was no sign of life. But as they moved closer to the center of the town, the buildings started looking better cared for and as though they may be in business, though they still didn't see any people.

A large, battered road-side sign read "Punchinello."

"Punchinello?" Johnny said from the backseat. "What a weird name."

"Hurry up and park," Candy whined, slapping the headrest. "I want to get out of this car!" She swooned dramatically against Greg.

Myra hesitated, not pulling into a parking spot right away. Her hackles were up. "I dunno, guys, something seems off…." She couldn't put her finger on it, but her gut told her to drive away.

"Ugh, don't be such a killjoy," Holly said, manually unlocking her door and hopping out, heading straight for the sidewalk. "C'mon, guys!" she hollered.

"Holly!" Myra exclaimed, but it was too late.

Greg and Candy poured out of the car too, leaving only Johnny in the car with her. He smiled apologetically. "Sorry, I guess we're exploring this town for a little bit."

With a heavy sigh, Myra went ahead and pulled off the road into a parking spot before shutting the car off. She slowly got out of the car, looking around and wondering why there weren't any people milling around when it was late afternoon.

"Hey," Johnny said, coming up beside her. "Haven't really gotten a chance to talk to just you, yet. Um, I hope you don't mind the three of us coming along on this trip. From what I can gather, Holly didn't exactly touch-base with you before inviting us."

Myra bit back an irritated retort. She knew being rude in return wouldn't help anything, and Johnny was the most pleasant of the tag-alongs, so she didn't want to be mean to him. Before she could come up with anything to say, though, Holly called to them from down the road.

"Hurry up, slowpokes! There's a really weird store over here!"

Johnny hurried off after her and the others, and Myra followed along more slowly. When she finally arrived at the storefront they'd disappeared into, she had to do a double take at the vision before her. The entire store was filled with nothing but clown paraphernalia. Clown statues, clown masks, clown paint, clown costumes, clown instruments. "What on earth?" she murmured to herself as she tentatively entered the store behind the others.

"Have you ever seen such a weird store?" Holly asked her, pawing through a rack of clown suits.

"Can't say that I have," Myra replied, lingering near the door.

They all jumped when a loud honk burst through the mostly quiet room around them. At the back of the store, near a door to presumably the backroom, stood a clown smiling widely, staring unblinking at them. He held in his hand a horn similar to one that could be found on a child's bike.

"Damn, dude," Greg said, "you nearly gave us a heart attack!"

The clown didn't say anything, didn't even move as he continued to stare at them. He honked his horn again. Did his eyes grow a little darker?

"Guys, I think we should go," Myra whispered.

"I think she's right," Johnny agreed.

Myra edged for the door, keeping her eyes so closely fixed on the clown that she nearly bumped into someone. She looked up to see who it was and jumped back in alarm when she realized it was yet another clown, this time a woman.

The lady clown stalked into the room, big smile on her face as she carefully looked at all of the others in the room. Then she reached out, snatched Candy's purse from her shoulder, and took off running out the door.

"Hey!" Candy yelled, Greg echoing her, as they tore after the clown. "Get back here, you clown freak!" Candy swung herself around the door frame in pursuit, Greg in step with her.

Johnny looked over at the other clown who still stood stock still. "What kind of crap are you guys pulling here?" he asked. "C'mon, girls," he said to Holly and Myra. "Let's go get them and get out of this town."

Johnny took the lead out of the store, Holly close on his heels, looking alarmed at the change in events. Myra followed more slowly, eyes transfixed on the clown who hadn't moved an inch since he'd stepped into the room. Finally, she ripped her gaze from him and bolted out of the store. Down the street, she saw Johnny and Holly running side-by-side, and ahead of them she just barely caught a glimpse of Greg and Candy slipping into a large, plain-looking building, presumably in pursuit of the purse thief.

Myra shook her head. This was insane. She turned her back and went in the opposite direction, hurrying to her car. She jumped in and locked the doors immediately before starting the engine. She put the car into drive and looked back up, this time to find that every store along the small-town main street had a clown standing in the doorway, all staring at her. One of the clowns was a small girl, probably no more than six-years-old. She had a big grin fixed on her face, and she waved at Myra and started skipping towards the car.

Myra jerked the car into drive and peeled out of the parallel parking space, racing away from those stores and towards the large building. By the time she made it there, the others weren't in sight. "No, no, no. Guys, where are you?" she muttered under her breath. She tapped the steering wheel nervously, trying to decide what to do. Every fiber of her being screamed at her to drive away, that it wasn't safe here. But she couldn't just leave the others behind…could she?

An agonized scream broke her from her thoughts, and she looked up to see Johnny exiting from a door in the side of the building, hobbling along painfully on a leg that was bleeding profusely. Yet another clown followed him out of the building, ax in hand, calmly pursuing his prey. As Myra stared in frozen shock, Johnny looked up and saw her. "Help me!" he cried out.

Without further thought, Myra floored the accelerator and rocketed towards the pursuing clown. Barely managing to dodge Johnny, she slammed into the clown, screaming as he bounced up onto the hood of her car, making eerie eye contact before she slammed on the brakes, sending him tumbling from the hood to the ground again. Before he could stand back up, she gunned it again, meaning to run him over. A loud popping noise as she bounced over his body, though, was her only clue that she'd made a grave error in judgment. Her car rolled to a sluggish stop, and the awkward angle she now set at could mean only one thing: one of the tires was popped.

She leapt out of the car and looked back at the clown on the ground. He was either dead or unconscious, and in his hand, blade tilted upwards, was the ax. She cursed herself for forgetting the bladed weapon. "Johnny!" she called, looking around for him. He'd fallen to a heap a few feet back, so she ran over to check on him. "What happened?" she asked. "Where are the others?"

Johnny shook his head, tears of pain and fear streaming down his face. "I don't know. There were so many of them in there. They swarmed us when we got in there. I think…I think Holly is…" he trailed off. "I don't know. I tried to run, but he got me. I shouldn't have left them." He trailed off, face in his hands.

Myra looked around helplessly and saw a group of clowns standing at the edge of town along the line of stores, the clowns who had watched her as she drove away. They didn't make any move to advance, but just their wide, staring eyes was enough to chill her soul. She looked back to the building the others had disappeared in. So far, no other clowns had come out in pursuit of Johnny, but he'd said the building was full of them. Why weren't they attacking? What was going on? Then her eyes fell back on her car. It was their only hope of escape, and only if she could get it working.

Setting her jaw determinedly, she dragged Johnny to his feet. "Okay, enough of that," she said. "I need to get the spare on this car, and I'll need you to help me." He tried to protest, but she dragged him roughly to the side of the car and set him next to the damaged tire. "I can change the tire," she said, waving off his protestations. "I just need you to keep track of the lug nuts while I do it. We can get out of this."

She hustled to the back of the jeep, popped open the hatch and tailgate, and began throwing their luggage out on the ground wildly, moving it all so that she could get to the spare tire and the kit in the bottom. Every few seconds she glanced up again. Why weren't they coming after them? She didn't understand. What was their game? Panic setting her heart to race, she got to work on the tire. Every second that her shaking hands fumbled at the task, she feared someone would suddenly come up and grab her. "How's it going, Johnny?" she asked as she took the first of the lug nuts from him once she got the spare settled into place. "Are you okay?" He was frighteningly pale. She knew she should find something to make a tourniquet to help control his bleeding, but she couldn't think through the fear to guess if any of them had packed a belt or anything like that.

"I'm really tired," he replied quietly. "I just want to sleep."

"No, hey!" Myra said, pausing her task with the lug nuts to lightly smack his cheeks. "You can't, I need you to stay awake." She looked around again. Still, the crowd of clowns watched from the town. Still, no clowns came pouring forth from the building. She set the last lug nut. "Okay, let's get you into the car." She pulled him to his feet again and helped him into the passenger seat. She ran around behind the car and spared just a few seconds digging through the suitcases until she found a scarf. It would have to do. "Here!" she shouted, tossing it into Johnny's lap. "Tie that around your leg. I'll help you do it better once I get us out of here."

He stared at her blankly as she started the car again. "Wait, what about the others?" he asked.

Myra shook her head, putting the car into drive. "We have to get out of here," she said.

Johnny moved sluggishly, attempting to tie the scarf around his thigh as she drove. "We can't just leave them behind," he protested.

"We don't know if they're even alive, Johnny!" she yelled. She looked over at him. "I can't go into that building to look for them. I *can't*. I'm too scared."

"But..." Johnny fell silent. "I guess I can't blame you," he finally said. He dropped his head into his hands.

Myra let the conversation drop and drove as fast as she dared on the rough dirt road, hands gripping the steering wheel tightly. She spared one glance up in the rear view mirror as she left. The crowd that had watched from the edge of the town was gone, but in the middle of the road, the clown she'd ran down with her car stood watching, casually twirling the ax in his hands as though it were a baton. Her heart jumped at the sight, and she pushed the car faster.

They drove in silence for a short time, following the winding dirt road through the desolate desert landscape. More than once they had to skirt around deep ruts in the road, and each time Myra braced herself for the vehicle to fall apart, but it all held together. They just had to hold on. They just needed to hang in there until the road connected back to a major highway. Then they could find police and get help. Johnny seemed to be absent of panic, sitting and dozing in and out next to her. Periodically, she'd snap her fingers or shake his arm to get him to come to. Around them, the sky slowly grew darker, and Myra began to dread figuring out how to navigate this terrain in the dark, but there was no way she'd ever feel safe just stopping out here in the middle of nowhere knowing those clowns could be anywhere.

Then, in the distance in the fading light, she caught a glimpse of civilization. A few scarce buildings, but surely they must be getting close to a highway! "Johnny," she said, "I think we're going to be okay. Look!" she said pointing.

Johnny roused himself again and looked out the glass. "What's that sign say?" he asked. "Turn up your lights."

Myra flipped on the high beams, and they both looked at the sign together.

"Punchinello...." Johnny said slowly.

"What?!" Myra cried. "It...it can't be! We've been driving for hours." She continued driving slowly forward, lost in utter shock. And just as earlier in the day, they slowly drove into a small town devoid of any signs of life despite the little shops lining each side of the road. Or rather, mostly devoid of life. Figures in the middle of the road forced her to a stop.

Johnny cried out in horror. Splayed out on the ground lay the butchered, bloodied bodies of both Greg and Candy. Standing calmly between their two bodies was a young female clown, grin stretched wide, eyes wide open and staring, face paint in harlequin style like the others. But she looked slightly different. She wasn't clad in a clown suit as many of the others had been. She was wearing normal clothes, clothes that Myra had seen before.

Myra gasped as recognition clicked. *Holly*. That was Holly standing in the street. But how? Why? What?! As Myra stared, clown-Holly raised her hand and slowly beckoned her forward. Myra shook her head. This wasn't happening. It *couldn't* be. So fixated was she on Holly, that she didn't notice the clowns approaching from the sides until hers and Johnny's car doors were yanked open. Glove-encased hands grasped at her arms and pulled her from the vehicle. "No, no!" she screamed, struggling fiercely, but to no avail. She looked over her shoulder and screamed again as she watched another clown sink a knife into Johnny's chest, killing him.

Then she was dragged away into one of the buildings and put into a chair with restraints. "Please, please let me go!" Myra screamed and sobbed. "We never meant to come here. This was a mistake! Just let me go, and I won't tell anyone about you, I swear!"

None of the clowns spoke to her, or each other for that matter. They just went about their business in the building around her until two turned towards her, something in their hands. She watched as they stalked slowly towards her, watched as they opened the lids to the small containers in their hand and dipped their fingers within, pulling them back to reveal white paint. Another hand gripped her by the hair, holding her in place, and she screamed one final time as they descended upon her.

Evil is as Evil Does

Mary awoke slowly as sun streaming through a crack in her curtains passed over her eyes. She stretched luxuriously and smiled. Today was going to be a fun day. She sat up and looked around. Everything was strictly neat, just how she liked it. From a glance at the clock, she saw that it was almost 8:30. Her husband, Dave, would already be hard at work, then. She'd wait until later in the day to check on him. That also meant her older daughter, Lilly, should be hard at work with her studies. They home-schooled her, but she was old enough now (already in high school, she could hardly believe it!) that she didn't need constant supervision. Mary frowned. Her daughter's quality of work had been slipping lately, though, and there had been some attitude too. She was going to have to have a talk with her. Her younger daughter, Cora, was also home schooled, but she did a much better job following the rules and staying on task. Mary smiled to herself. She knew it really wasn't right to have a favorite, but there was no doubt in her mind that hers was Cora. She wondered if Dave had a favorite. He worked so much, he barely saw the girls, but she suspected he favored Lilly.

Finally, she climbed out of bed and worked through her morning routine, getting ready for the day. She made up her face until she was satisfied with the—in her humble opinion—gorgeous appearance, selected attractive clothes that were still appropriate for a day out, and then left her room to fix herself breakfast. She found Cora sitting at the kitchen table, working away in her arithmetic workbook. "Good morning, Cora," she said as she entered the room. "How goes your studies?"

"Good," Cora said, not looking up from the page of simple multiplication that she worked on.

Mary got out a granola bar and nibbled at it while watching her daughter meticulously work through each equation on the page. When she finished, she said, "Let me take a look at how you did."

Cora passed over the booklet and waited patiently while her mother scanned through all of the math problems.

Mary looked up, a severe look on her face. "These are…" she let her face break into a smile, "all correct! Perfect job, Cora."

Cora grinned. "Thanks!"

Mary finished the last bite of her granola bar and threw the wrapper into the trash can. "Okay, sweetheart. I'm going out for a while with my friend Julie. I'm leaving you in charge," she said with a smile and a wink.

"Okay," Cora replied. "Have fun!"

~~~

Thirty minutes later, Mary was sitting in her car, parked along the curb in the downtown shopping district and waiting for Julie to text her that she'd arrived too. Their plans were to visit a variety of stores and then grab a light lunch before calling it a day. Julie's text came in, so Mary got out of her car and walked to the first store they'd agreed to shop at. They spent some time perusing several stores, each choosing a few items to buy until they were laden down with multiple bags each. After depositing the bags in their cars, they headed to a street-side cafe for lunch.

"So, how is Dave doing?" Julie asked, taking a sip of the iced tea she'd ordered.

"Oh, you know," Mary said with a sigh. "Always working like usual. It feels like I hardly ever see him, but he does do such a good job supporting me and the girls."

Julie gave her a sympathetic smile. "I know what it's like living with a workaholic husband. It'd be nice if they'd take just one day off here and there to spend with us. At least you have your girls, though. All I have are my dogs. What are Lilly and Cora up to? Did Lilly decide to join in any activities this year?"

Mary shook her head disappointedly. "No, she hasn't. I worry about that girl. She's already 16-years-old, you know? But I can't get her interested in trying any kind of activity. All she wants to do is sit around in her room sulking. I just don't know where all that attitude comes from. Maybe it would be easier if she were in school with other kids, but she had such major behavioral issues when she was little, we just had to keep her home for her own good and everyone else's."

Julie reached out and patted her friend's hand. "Maybe the attitude issues are just a phase. The teenage years are hard, as I remember." She half-smiled at her own joke. "I'm glad for you that you have Cora, at least."

Mary's face visibly brightened at Cora's name. "Yes, she really is such a good girl. She's so much like me, and she's so agreeable and good at following the house rules. Honestly, I wish she were the older sister. She'd be a good role model for Lilly." She shook her head and rubbed her neck. "Ugh, enough depressing talk," she said. "Tell me more about how your little mangy mutts are doing." She stuck her tongue out to soften the blow of the insult.

They finished their meal, Julie spending entirely too much time gushing about the escapades of little Hansel and Gretel, her two Pomeranians, but Mary politely listened to it all. After all, it was her own fault since she switched the conversation to them. And it was good for Julie to have someone human to talk to for once. As they gathered their purses and paid the bill, Julie glance over across the street, and a girlish grin crossed her face. "Hey, look over there, Mary. A fortune teller! C'mon, let's go get your fortune told."

"What?" Mary exclaimed. "Why mine?"

"Because," Julie answered, already tugging on Mary's arm, "I have the distinct impression that you've never done this before, and it's lots of fun. You just *have* to do it," she said exaggeratedly.

"I dunno," Mary chuckled, letting Julie tug her along. "Isn't this all kind of hokey?"

"Of *course* it's hokey. That's what makes it fun!" Julie kept on dragging Mary behind her until she got her into the dimly lit building. They found themselves in a small lobby with a couple of chairs. At the back of the room was a doorway covered in gossamer curtains.

As they entered, a woman dressed up in a full-on, cliche fortuneteller costume rose to greet them. "Good afternoon," she greeted solemnly.

"Hi there," Julie said brightly. "My friend would like to get her fortune told."

"Very well," the woman said, gesturing to the door to the back. They passed through the curtain and took a seat at a small table covered in a velvet cloth that draped all the way to the floor.

On display in the center of the table was a large crystal ball. "It's thirty dollars for a reading," the woman said as she sat down. She held out her hand, waiting for the payment before saying anything further.

Mary made a slight face, but still went ahead and pulled the money from her wallet and handed it over.

After slipping the money somewhere on her person, the fortune teller took a deep breath and let it out slowly before reaching out and lightly touching the crystal ball, looking at it intensely. She stared for a few moments, not saying anything, but then she gasped and lurched back in her seat. She looked up at Mary, eyes wide in terror.

"What?" Mary asked, mildly alarmed. "What do you see?" Was it bad news? Did the fortuneteller foresee some tragic event, perhaps the death of her husband?

"You…" the fortuneteller pointed a shaking finger at Mary. "You're evil. Pure evil." Her eyes were wide with fear. "You need to leave," she said, standing up so suddenly she nearly overturned her chair. "Right now."

Mary looked at Julie, flabbergasted.

Julie gaped in shock at the fortuneteller, but finally her shock changed to anger. "How dare you," she said. "My friend is having a stressful time, so I thought we could have some fun getting a fortune, and you decide to pull this crazy scheme on us?"

The fortuneteller briefly glanced at Julie before returning her attention to Mary, as though she were afraid of taking her eyes off of her. "It's not a scheme. I meant what I said. I want you both out of my shop." Her fear was waning and courage was building.

Julie stood up, pulling Mary up with her. "You have no idea

what you're talking about. Mary is the nicest person I know. She supports and cherishes a man who works hard all day long for her, and she does everything she can to help her two daughters be the best they can be. She is the very backbone of her family."

The fortuneteller looked at her sharply. "Perception and what is often aren't the same."

"This is ridiculous. I'm so sorry, Mary. Let's just get out of here." Julie pivoted and hurried through the curtains.

Mary lingered for a moment, studying the fortuneteller, who kept her eyes raptly on her. Mary jerked forward suddenly, and the fortuneteller flinched back, causing Mary to laugh. She turned and walked for the curtained doorway, but stopped to look over her shoulder. "You know," Mary said, "you're crazy if you think one little peek into that crystal ball tells you the whole story. I'm a good person, and I do everything in my power to make people be the best they can at their roles, to excel in life as nature intends. If I'm 'evil,' then love is evil, because every one of my actions is driven by my love for my family and my desire to see them do well." Then she strode away, not seeing the fortuneteller immediately retrieve sage to burn to cleanse her studio.

Once they were outside, Julie turned to Mary again. "Gosh, Mary, I really am so sorry. This was such a bad idea."

Mary patted Julie on the shoulder. "Don't worry about it, dear. It's all harmless. On that note, though, I think I'm going to head home now. I need to check in on my girls to see how they're doing with their studies and start preparing dinner for them."

The two women said their farewells and then headed for their cars to go home.

~~~

When she arrived home, Mary carried all of her bags to her bedroom, and then she went and found Cora in the den where she was watching cartoons. "Hey, sweetie," she said, petting her hair. "Did you finish all of your school work?"

"Yes, it's all sitting on the kitchen table."

"And how did things go here? Any issues?"

Cora shrugged. "Not really. Lilly screamed for a little while, and Daddy did try to talk to me once, but I just ignored him, just like you always say to."

Mary groaned inwardly, but praised her daughter for being good and following the rules. Honestly, why was it so hard for the other two to understand that she had set up everything in their lives to be perfect for what they needed if only they'd toe the line? "I'm going to go make dinner soon, and I'll call you when it's ready. Enjoy your show!"

Mary headed back up to the kitchen and put together a pasta casserole, putting it in the over before heading down the hall to check on her other two family members. First, she stopped at Lilly's room, knocking twice before opening the door. In a flurry of movement, her daughter rushed at her, but was caught short by a chain that was shackled around her wrist and hooked into the ground in the far corner of the room.

"Let me out of here!" her daughter cried. "You can't just keep me in her all the time!"

Mary sighed and shook her head. "Did you do any of your schoolwork today?"

Lilly screamed like a banshee. "Please, just let me out of this room!"

Mary frowned. "Lilly, I asked you a question."

"Ugh, no! I didn't do any of it. I'm not doing anything you ask until you let me go. I'm not some dog you can keep chained up in the yard all day!"

Mary sighed and rubbed her temples. "Young lady, there is hardly any cause for these hysterics. You're in the situation you're in because of your own actions. You misbehave, act out, and don't follow rules. I can't trust you outside of this room. Until you learn to straighten up, do your schoolwork, and not backtalk me, you will remain in this room forever."

Lilly tried to lash out at her mother with her free hand, but Mary caught her wrist in an unnervingly strong grip. "I will bring you some dinner in a little while. In the meantime," she squeezed Lilly's wrist until she whimpered from the pain, "do. your. school work." Then she pushed Lilly back and slammed the door in her face. Lilly continued screaming from insider her room, but Mary tuned her out. She wasn't going to suffer Lilly's tantrums.

Instead, she stepped across the hall to her husband's room and entered, again, knocking twice first. If nothing else, she was always polite. Her husband looked up at her with tired eyes as she entered the brightly lit room. The rhythmic sound of a sewing machine came to a stop as she stepped into the room, and she reached down to begin sorting through the pile of items he'd sewn that day. "How did it go today, Dave? Productive day?"

"Um, yes, I think so," Dave said quietly, watching her nervously as she counted through the stock.

"Hmmm," Mary said. "You're good on shirts, pants, and scarves, but it looks like we'll need two more blankets before you finish tonight to meet the quota we promised."

Dave sighed and rubbed his eyes. "Honey, can we please lower our quota moving forward? I've been at this for almost twelve hours and it's just.…" he trailed off as she glared at him. "Uh, not that it's too much," he stammered. "It's just, I never get to see you or the girls. Are they okay? I thought I heard Lilly screaming earlier."

"We've been over this. The girls are my responsibility as the homemaker, Dave," Mary said quietly. "You should be keeping your mind on your responsibility, earning the income to support our household. That's your role in this family."

"But, Mary, can't I please see the girls for just a few minutes?" He shifted in his chair, the rattle of a chain dragging across the ground sounding as he moved.

"Cora tells me that you already tried talking to her today while I wasn't here," Mary said accusingly. "You probably would have finished the quota before I checked in if you'd stayed focused. Honestly, Dave, I don't understand why you struggle with this so much."

Dave's breath hitched in his chest as he fought back tears. "Oh please, please just let me out of this room, even for just a few hours. There's not even a window. I haven't seen the sun in so long, Mary!"

"There's no window because you're too easily distracted, Dave. Now get back to work," she said, pointing at the sewing machine, "and I'll bring you your dinner soon."

"No, Mary. Mary wait!"

But she'd closed the door in his face and walked away. Without her there, he'd be able to focus and finish his work for the day. When she returned the kitchen, she picked up the mail and sorted through it all. She sighed when she came across a card addressed to her husband. She opened it and read through it. Another condolences card for him because his father had died about a week ago. Dave didn't know that, of course. Goodness, he didn't have the emotional fortitude to withstand such a loss, not when he started falling apart at the seams just because she asked him to keep himself on the task at hand. No, better for him to remain in the dark on such an unfortunate turn of events.

That was her burden to bear. She was the backbone of her family, holding it all together and supporting it through life's adversities. And no matter what, whatever it took, she would see that everything stayed smooth and perfect, as it should be.

Invitation

Judy stumbled through the halls of her middle school, buffeted around by other students as she tried to make her way to the cafeteria for lunch. She was a small girl that was easily unnoticed, but she was lucky enough that one of the more popular girls, Morgan, and her friend Chelsea had decided to let her sit with them at lunch this semester! Especially lucky since her best (a basically only) friend since first grade had just moved away a few months ago, leaving her essentially friendless. Finally, she made it, dropping breathlessly into a seat next to Morgan as she sat her lunch box on the table before her. "Hi, guys," she said once she'd caught her breath.

Morgan and Chelsea both replied in kind, smiling at her slyly.

Judy blinked. "What's up with you two?" she asked.

Morgan slid a little closer. "Do you think your mom would let you come spend the night at my house tonight?"

Judy frowned as she pulled her sandwich from her lunch box. It was a Friday, so her mom probably would allow it since they didn't have school the next day, but the way Morgan was acting was creeping her out. Still, she didn't want to get on her new friend's bad side, so she said, "Yeah, I guess. Why?"

Chelsea grinned largely. "Morgan found something *really* cool that we want to check out. And we want you to see it too."

"What is it?"

"An old video tape," Morgan said smugly. "Got it from a friend of a friend of a friend. It's a bunch of old recordings of *real* seances, exorcisms, rituals, and stuff like that. Supposed to be super scary." She waggled her eyebrows at Judy. "They say it's like the movie's...cursed." She shifted her voice dramatically, poking fun at the idea.

Judy felt her stomach sink. She wasn't really into horror, and something supposedly real sounded horrifying. "I don't know...." she said, trailing off.

"Oh c'mon," Morgan scoffed. "Don't be such a chicken. It'll be fun!"

"Yeah. It *is* Halloween, after all," Chelsea added. "Spooky season!"

"I..." Judy stared at her peanut-butter and jelly sandwich for a moment. "Fine, I'll get my mom to let me come over," she finally relented. She knew she'd never live it down if she was too scared to come over.

"Good," Morgan said smoothly, leaning back casually now that she'd gotten her way.

~~~

Later that night, after a successful talk with her mother, Judy found herself at Morgan's house. She and Morgan sat at the breakfast bar in the kitchen drinking soda and eating popcorn as they waited for Chelsea to arrive. While they chatted and ate, Morgan's mom bustled around the kitchen taking care of a week's worth of dishes and cleaning. She was divorced and worked long hours as an emergency room doctor, so unless Morgan helped out, which she rarely did, she often found herself behind keeping up with the household chores. "What are you girls planning to do tonight?" she asked as she worked.

"Oh you know," Morgan replied casually, "just hanging out. Probably going to watch a movie. Stuff like that."

Her mom glanced her way as she rinsed out the sponge and dropped it on the counter. "No horror movies, Morgan. I don't need a passel of panicky teens on my hands tonight."

Morgan rolled her eyes. "As if, Mom. We're not babies."

"I mean it, Morgan." Her mom lingered in the doorway on her way out of the kitchen, clearly expecting a response.

"Fine, no horror flicks," Morgan replied.

As her mom walked away satisfied, Judy felt a small amount of hope bubble within her. Maybe they wouldn't watch that video now.

But her hopes were quickly dashed as Morgan raise her hand from where she'd been hiding it under the counter to show that her fingers were crossed. "Not a lie if the fingers are crossed," she said triumphantly. "C'mon, let's go to the basement and get ready while we wait on Chelsea." As they left through the kitchen into the living room, the phone rang. Morgan picked it up, and her eyes narrowed. "Really, Chelsea? You know you're supposed to come over to my house and you go and get yourself grounded?" She paused a moment to listen to Chelsea. "Yeah, whatever. Thanks a lot," she muttered, hanging up the phone without further ado.

"Not coming?" Judy asked timidly.

"No," Morgan said disgustedly. "And I'll bet she did it on purpose because she chickened out on watching the tape." She sighed. "Whatever, let's get it going."

Judy followed Morgan to the basement and watched as she dimmed the lights and turned on the TV and sound system.

INVITATION

She wanted so badly to say that she didn't want to watch the movie either, but it was obvious that Morgan was angry with Chelsea, and she really didn't want to ostracize herself from the only friends she had. She bit her lip and curled into a ball on the couch as Morgan came back to join her, remote in hand.

"Alright, here we go!" Morgan said eagerly.

~~~

Ninety minutes later, Judy was shaken to her core. The video certainly seemed real. No Hollywood-ized editing, no soundtrack. It just looked like recordings done with handheld video cameras. The videos were less exaggerated than she was used to seeing in horror flicks, but the lack of presentation really drove home the realistic nature of the videos and chilled her to the bone. And the sounds, some of the sounds coming from the speakers were truly horrific. Even Morgan looked slightly shaken as she got up to take the tape out and turn of the electronic equipment. Judy was absolutely petrified. She knew with certainty she would not be able to sleep at all that night, and she didn't want to stay over anymore. But she couldn't admit that to Morgan either. She needed help. And then an idea came to her.

"Um, I'm gonna go to the bathroom. Be right back." Judy slipped away toward the bathroom, but on her way, she grabbed the cordless phone from the living room. While locked in the bathroom, she called her house. It was around 10:00 p.m., so late, but not unforgivably so. "Hi, Mom?" she whispered into the phone. "I'm sorry to call so late, but I want to come home." Her mom sounded confused, but said she'd come right away. "No, wait!" Judy said. "I don't want Morgan to know I called you. Please, *please,* call and make up some reason that I have to go home. Please." Judy breathed a sigh of relief when her mom agreed, and she hurried back out to deposit the phone before she was found with it.

She rejoined Morgan in the basement, and a few moments later, the phone rang. In the distance, she heard Morgan's mom answer it, and then she came to find them in the basement. "Sorry to break up your fun, girls," she said, "but Judy's mom just called. Something came up, and Judy has to go home now."

"Aw, really?" Judy said, trying to feign disappointment. She didn't know how successful she was, and she didn't really care either. She just wanted to go home where her parents wouldn't look down on her for being afraid of a spooky movie.

Morgan was obviously upset. "First Chelsea and now you," she said, pouting. "So much for a fun weekend." She ignored any further comments from Judy or her mother and just went to her room, leaving Judy alone in the living room to wait for her mom.

It didn't take long until she arrived, and Judy said goodbye to Morgan's mom and asked her to tell Morgan she was sorry. Morgan's mom brushed her comment aside. "She's a big girl, or she should be anyway. She'll get over it. Have a good weekend, dear."

And so Judy left, explaining to her mom what had happened and trying to put the movie out of her mind.

~~~

Morgan sighed, alone in her room as she started to get ready for bed. She usually didn't go to sleep so early on a Friday, but with both of her friends canceling on her, she felt too bummed to do anything else. But sleep didn't really sound appealing either; the video she'd watched with Judy had disturbed her, and she was particularly angry that Judy was gone because now she didn't have someone to lean on to deal with that unease. It wasn't like she could fess up to her mom about what she watched after her mom made a whole case about not watching scary movies.

A short while after she heard Judy leave, the phone rang again, and a few minutes later, her mom opened her bedroom door while in the process of putting on her coat. "Bad news, sweetheart. There's been a multiple car accident out on the interstate, so they're calling us all in to deal with multiple casualties. I'll check in on you as soon as I can, but for now, hold the fort." She turned and headed for the garage.

Morgan's heart jumped to her throat. She didn't want to be left alone! Not after watching that movie. "Wait," she said, following her mom. "Do you really have to go? I don't really want to be…by myself."

Her mom frowned suspiciously, paused in the action of opening the door to the garage. "You're usually so eager for a chance to stay home alone." Realization dawned on her face. "You watched something scary, didn't you."

Morgan thought about lying, but was too tired to carry on the charade. "Yes," she sighed.

Her mom shrugged her shoulders. "I warned you not to. I have to go help all of those people, so you're on your own tonight. You're the one who wanted to watch the movie; figure out a way to deal with it." And then she was gone, leaving Morgan an upset mess.

The immediate silence after her mom drove away was unsettling. Morgan quickly went through the whole house turning on all of the lights. If her mom wouldn't be sympathetic to her, then she could deal with the spike in the electricity bill. Once all of the lights were on, she sat uncomfortably on the couch in the living room with a magazine, trying to distract herself. It wasn't working. She kept thinking she heard sounds in the house. A creak here, a pop there. The lights overhead flickered, and she clutched her magazine tighter. Then downstairs, the TV turned on. Morgan jumped in alarm. "Who's there?" she shrieked in a strangled voice.

No one responded, but she distinctly heard the sounds of the video from before starting again. But that was impossible. She'd removed the tape from the VCR, she knew it! "What's going on?" she whispered to herself. Behind her, she heard a voice whisper her name. She screamed and turned around, but nothing was there. Then she thought she felt a hand stroke her shoulder. Again she screamed and pulled away, but there was nothing there. She started to cry then. What was happening?

"So nice of you to invite us in," a cruel voice whispered from the void.

"No!" Morgan screamed, turning left and right, trying to find the source of the voice. "Leave me alone!"

The voice tutted. "Not until we get what we came for."

Morgan tried to run, but the whole house seemed to shake around her like there was an earthquake or something. She tried to reach for the front door, but it appeared to melt before her eyes into nothing but a wall. She scrabbled at the surface with her nails, but she couldn't gain any purchase. Invisible hands grasped at her again, and she screamed and flailed, but nothing she did worked. And then suddenly, she fell silent.

Outside, people went about their late-night activities none the wiser. No sound came from the house, and no lights either; the residents must be in bed asleep.

INVITATION

~~~

By Monday morning, Judy was a nervous wreck. She's tried calling Morgan a few times over the weekend but got no answer, and Morgan didn't return her calls. Did Morgan somehow guess that Judy had been the one who chose to leave rather than her mother making that decision? Or was she just mad regardless? Had she just lost another friend? Judy felt miserable and hated herself. As soon as she'd gotten home, the fear that she'd felt from watching that video had begun waning, and by the end of the weekend it was gone. She felt like a fool. Because of a few jitters, she'd probably just ruined their relationship.

When she got to school, she walked dejectedly down the hall, not looking anyone in the eye as she made her way for her locker, and she jumped a mile when someone reached out and grabbed her arm.

"Hey," Chelsea said. "How did the sleepover go? Was Morgan really mad at me? I tried calling her later during the weekend but never could get a hold of her."

Judy blinked at her. "She wouldn't talk to you either?"

"What do you mean?" Chelsea asked.

Judy sighed. "My mom called and made me leave before spending the night because some things came up, and Morgan got upset. I couldn't talk to her all weekend either."

"Ah jeez," Chelsea grumbled, rolling her eyes. "She always gets moody like this. Probably won't forgive us until we grovel at her feet enough to satisfy her ego."

Judy was surprised to hear Chelsea talk that way. She'd never seen the other two girls fight before.

"Well," Chelsea continued, "I'm going to see if I can find her before first period. See you later, Judy."

Judy went on ahead to her class. As much as it sucked that Morgan was mad at them, she was glad that she wasn't the only one in the doghouse. Hopefully she and Chelsea would be able to mollify her soon. Judy didn't have any classes with Morgan until after lunch, so she probably wouldn't see her before then. She wondered if Chelsea was successful in finding her before school started.

During her third class, Judy felt her cell phone buzz from an incoming text. After a glance to make sure the teacher wasn't looking her way, Judy looked at the message. "Meet us in the bathroom. Now," it read. It was from Morgan. Maybe Chelsea had already sweet talked her into forgiving them?

Judy was reluctant to get caught skipping class, but she didn't want to make Morgan mad again either. And besides, there technically wasn't a rule about kids going to the bathroom during class. She raised her hand and got permission to use the restroom. There were two bathrooms she could choose from. One was much larger and more frequented, and the other was smaller and kind of out of the way from most of the classrooms, tucked into an alcove near the art classrooms and the gym. That was probably where Morgan expected them to meet.

Judy headed for that one and stepped inside. She was the first to arrive, it seemed. She stood awkwardly waiting, grimacing each time the old fluorescent light overhead flickered. Then a sound, a faint slumping, came from the far stall, startling Judy. She hadn't thoroughly checked each stall, but she had thought she was alone. Cautiously, she edged along the front of the stalls and pushed open the last door. Inside, sitting slumped atop the toilet, was Chelsea. She looked dazed, and not at all with it. Possibly not even alive. Judy covered her mouth with her hands, eyes wide with shock as she stared. Then she heard the door to the bathroom open behind her.

"Hello, *friend*," a voice said. "We did so miss you the other night." The voice was eerie, sounding both like and unlike Morgan. Judy slowly turned to find her standing there blocking the door, but her eyes were burning red. "You missed out on all the fun," Morgan continued, her voice now no longer her own, "but we will rectify that." Then she closed the bathroom door with a terminal snap.

Daughter Dearest

Jack Brown and his wife Alice puttered around their kitchen one late afternoon, cleaning up the kitchen after the dinner they'd just eaten. Alice rinsed the dishes and loaded the dishwasher while Jack wiped down the counters and table. They didn't talk, having already discussed their days over their meal. They just work in familiar, companionable silence, completely unaware of the sudden shift their evening was about to take.

The sound of a ringing phone ripped through the silence, startling both of them. They chuckled sheepishly at each other, and Jack said, "I'll get that," throwing the sponge onto the counter as he headed for the phone in the living room. "Hello?" he answered.

"Hi, Daddy," said a voice on the other end. It sounded like a teenage girl.

"Sorry, kid," Jack said. "You've got the wrong number." He hung up the phone and started to head back for the kitchen, but the phone rang again. Frowning, Jack answered it again. "Hello?"

"Daddy, that wasn't very nice. Why did you hang up on me?" the sugary sweet voice asked.

Jack shifted his feet in annoyance. "I told you, kid, you have the wrong number. I don't have any kids." He started to lower the phone, but before he could hang up, her voice came through again.

"Well not anymore, but you did once."

Jack's eyes widened, and his grip tightened on the phone. "What did you say?"

The girl giggled. "Oh come on, Daddy, don't tell me you've forgotten me! How could you? After all, you were the last thing I saw before—"

Jack slammed the phone down into the cradle, his breathing heavy. "What's going on?" he muttered to himself. He backed away from the phone, eyes fixed on it as if it were a snake. He jumped when his wife came up behind him and touched his shoulder.

"Good grief!" Alice exclaimed at his reaction, shrinking away from him. "Jack, what's wrong? Who was that on the phone?"

Jack shook his head. "Nothing, it was no one." As soon as the words left his mouth, the phone rang again. "Don't answer that!" he yelled, eyes wide.

Alice gave him a strange look. "What has gotten into you, Jack?" she asked, eyeing him warily as she approached the phone.

"I said don't answer!" Jack yelled again, grabbing at her arm to hold her back, but she pulled away.

"Jack, it could be my mother. You *know* she's still recovering from her surgery." She picked up the phone. "Hello?"

"Hi, Mommy!" said a chipper voice on the other side.

"Oh, I'm sorry, honey, you have a wrong number." Alice paused, waiting for the girl to apologize and hang up.

"Oh, not you too, Mommy," the voice whined. "Daddy keeps pretending like he doesn't remember me too. I thought for sure you wouldn't do that."

Alice frowned and looked over at Jack, who stood rigid, his face a sickly pale color. "Now see here, young lady," she said, turning stern. "I don't know what kind of game you're trying to play, but my husband and I don't have any children. Now hang up that phone and do not call us again." Despite the finality in her tone, she hesitated before dropping the phone.

The girl sighed. "Wow, Mommy, that's just too mean. How can you be so cruel to your beautiful little baby, Jane?"

Alice dropped the phone and turned to her husband. "What the hell is that?!" she exclaimed, pointing at the phone. "Why is some girl calling us and saying that she's Jane?"

Now that his wife was panicking, Jack managed to find some composure. "Calm down, honey," he said, placing the phone back into the cradle before reaching out and pulling her into a hug. "It's probably just some dumb teenager showing off for her friends. Let's just ignore it and watch some TV."

No sooner were the words out of his mouth than the phone rang again. Both of them jumped, clinging to each other as they stared at the phone. Finally, Jack came to his senses, and he yanked the phone from the cradle. "Stop calling us, you little bitch!" he snarled into the receiver. "What?" He blanched and covered his face with his hand. "Oh, I'm...I'm so sorry, Helen. Just a moment." He turned to his wife. "It's your mom," he mumbled.

Alice glared at Jack and took the phone, taking it into the kitchen as she said, "Hi, Mom. No no, everything's fine. Jack's just upset about a prank call from earlier. He thought you were someone else."

Her voice faded as she left the room, and Jack collapsed tiredly onto the couch. He hoped his wife would stay on the phone for a long time, long enough for the prankster to get bored of the busy tone and leave them alone. They didn't need any memories of…before.

He turned the TV on, looking for anything to watch to take his mind off the odd calls. Mindlessly, he switched through the channels, pausing here and there, looking for something interesting to watch, anything to free him from the eerie feeling that still sat deep in his gut. The channels flashed before his eyes: a little girl and her dad walking in a park, a father holding his newborn baby and crying tears of joy, a father walking his daughter down the aisle at her wedding, a little girl taking her first steps and shuffling into her father's waiting arms. With growing unease, he noticed the pattern in the programming.

His wife returned and sat next to him after hanging up the phone; she was saying something about her mother's condition, but he didn't listen. The sport's channel, that would be fine. He typed in the channel number by memory, and up popped footage of a baseball game. He only got a few seconds of players running around on the field before the footage cut away to a reporter standing next to a man holding a small girl. It was her first ballgame. Jack switched off the TV and threw the remote. "This is crazy!"

His wife looked at him in alarm. "Jack, what on—"

The phone rang again.

They both stared at it before Alice timidly reached out and answered it, putting it on speaker phone. "Daddy, what's the matter?" the girl said through the phone. "I thought TV was your favorite pastime."

Jack clenched his fists to keep them from shaking. "Who are you?" he demanded.

The girl giggled again. "I've already told you guys, I'm Jane!"

Alice covered her mouth. "This is impossible," she said quietly.

The girl giggled again, but this time it lacked the cutesy nature from before. "You would think so, wouldn't you, Mommy?"

Alice and Jack looked at each other from across the couch, both unable to find words to explain what was happening.

"I was so hopeful that the two of you had changed since we last saw each other," Jane continued. "After all, you both did smile ever so sweetly at me just before Daddy held the pillow over my face."

Alice sobbed, and Jack grew ever paler.

"All these years, all fifteen years, I've been trying to understand why you would do it." All cheer had since vanished from her voice, leaving an unsettling calm in its wake. "I never could find the reason, but I did decide that it must have been a hard decision. I mean, you both smiled so wonderfully at me, I just knew how much you loved me. I knew that you wanted me to remember that love even after the end."

Jack looked around. Was the room darker than it had been before?

"And so…" The voice continued, but it was no longer coming from the phone. They both looked over by the front door, and Alice screamed as a shadowy figure faded into view. The distorted figure flickered and was difficult to make out, but it was the size of a teen girl who looked vaguely like what Alice may have grown up to become, except for her eyes, which were nothing more than dark, abyssal pits. "And so," she repeated, "I decided to do what any loving daughter should do and grant you your wish."

"Our wish?" Alice managed to whisper. She reached a shaky hand for Jack who, despite his trembling legs, managed to rise and move to stand protectively before her.

"You know, *mommy*," the revenant crooned. "You want us all

to be a family again. Mommy, Daddy, and baby-dearest. Why else would you have smiled at me as you did right before you smothered the life from me than if you loved me with all your heart and wanted to shield me from your regretful despair?" She floated closer to them. "Of course what you really want is for us all to be together again. Forever."

"No, please," Jack said, his voice cracking from strain. "Don't hurt us. A-at least don't hurt your mother. What we did…it was my idea. And it was my hands that did it."

The shadowy figure seemed to flair for a moment as if agitated, causing Jack to flinch away, but it simmered back down. "Why did you do it?" she suddenly asked. "I've wondered so long; I always wanted to know the real reason."

Jack chewed the inside of his cheek, unsure of how to answer. Did he try to come up with a lie, something to make them look tragically heroic? He couldn't come up with anything plausible. And somehow, he felt like the figure already knew the answer. Was this a test? If he spoke the truth, if he admitted their wrongs, would that save them? If he apologized, would that make everything better? "…Alice and I…we didn't have much money. We didn't know how we would pay our bills, keep our house, stuff like that. And then with another life to care for…it was just too much, honey." He hesitated, trying to get a sense of emotion from the dark figure before him, but he couldn't get anything. "We had taken a life insurance policy out on you, and after waiting enough time to not look suspicious, we took your life."

The figure flared again, so Jack hurried to keep talking. "But, Jane, listen, we are so sorry." He squeezed his wife's hand, urging her to join in.

"Oh yes," she said, cottoning onto his plan, "we're so sorry, sweetheart. We didn't want to lose you, but we had no other choice! We had to take care of each other."

The figure was silent for a moment, and both Alice and Jack stood frozen, hand-in-hand as they awaited the outcome. "You really think a simple 'sorry' makes up for what you did?" the voice asked, somehow even colder still. It no longer sounded anything like a young teenage girl, nor did the figure look like one. It had grown larger, now a hulking menace.

"Who…who are you?" Jack asked. "You're not Jane, are you?" He heard Alice gasp behind him.

"No, I'm not," the figure replied. It shifted, and the darkness of it seemed to brush aside, almost like a cloak being pushed back, and a small, shimmering white light appeared. It shown blindingly before their eyes before taking on the appearance of a small infant held in the crook of a shadowy arm. "This is Jane, unchanged since her death, and due to my protection, uncorrupted by the evils of *our* world, and untainted by your hateful actions."

"N-no," Jack sputtered. "We…we didn't hate…we just tried to…"

The figure billowed violently. "Silence, mortal!" the shadow rumbled. "No feeble excuse will ever save your wretched souls."

Jack and Alice clung to each other, freely crying now as the shadow swelled before them, a palatable wrath exuding from it.

"Given the purity and simplicity of one so young, it took much time to learn from her what had happened to her. But now I know, and I know the pain and betrayal that she felt." The shadows gently closed around the ball of light again, shielding it from the world. "So now you will pay for your actions."

"No, please!" both Jack and Alice screamed in unison. But it was far too late. There was a sound like the snapping of fingers, and the figure faded from view, Jane's spirit fading with it. For a moment, silence hung heavily in the room. Then with a deafening rush, dark and evil spirits materialized, filling every inch of the living room before ravaging the couple. They tried to hold on to each other, but they were ripped apart. The spirits reached within them, seizing their very souls, shredding and sundering, and finally dragging them to unknown depths of deepest, darkest suffering, where they were to toil for eternity, paying for their selfish choice, alone.

Infection

"Guys, I don't think we should be doing this," Nate whined as he followed the three older boys along the overgrown forest path. "We're not supposed to be over here."

His big brother Rory glanced over his shoulder. "We're just going to take a look. Just go home if you're going to be a baby about it," he said. "But you'd better not say anything to Mom."

Nate's lower lip trembled slightly, but he curled his little fists and soldiered on. He wasn't a baby. He would prove it! He stumbled over a tree root as he worked extra hard to keep up with the bigger boys' larger strides.

Even though the weatherman had promised rain later in the day, above them the blue sky was bright and full of cheerful, puffy white clouds. Not at all the kind of day one would associate with going to "the forbidden zone." Rory and his friends had been plotting this for a long time, waiting for the perfect time when they could all be together and their parents be none the wiser of their whereabouts, and it finally happened. The next town over was hosting a visiting carnival, and their parents had all given them permission to walk over and spend the day there, giving them a whole day to their mission.

There wasn't much of anything interesting to the little mining town they lived in but for one thing: occasionally, people would just suddenly go missing without a trace, but none of the adults seemed to care. Or rather, it was like all the adults *knew* what had happened and just wouldn't talk about it. It was always entire households that would vanish, and then the town would just calmly take possession of the homes and belongings, and no one would bat an eye. In addition to these random disappearances that even the sheriff and his deputies weren't concerned about, there was also a remote side of town the adults had labeled "the forbidden zone," and children were rigorously coached from birth never to go over there.

Nate, only eight-years-old, had always been a pretty well-behaved kid, always minding what his mother and father told him to do. Rory, on the other hand, had been a handful for his parents practically from day one. Always fussy when he was little turned always obstinate as he got older. Never wanting to follows the rules for the sake of being compliant, always having to question everything. And now, he had himself a crew of like-minded friends who all felt the same way about the forbidden zone: just what was so important that needed to be hidden?

And so it was that they found themselves at a tall chain-length fence topped with razor wire, which formed the perimeter of the forbidden zone. "Alright, boys," Rory's best friend Zach said. "We're here. Time to let ourselves in." He pulled a pair of bolt cutters from his backpack and went to work on the fence while the other boys kept watch.

The third boy, Beau, stretched while waiting. "What do you guys think we're gonna find in there?" he asked.

"I'll bet it's a literal gold mine," Rory said. "They've got us all thinking that all they mine here is coal, but I'll bet they found gold too and they're keeping it hidden so that they don't have to share the riches."

Nate stared wide-eyed at his brother. "Wow, you really think?"

Beau snorted. "What're you impressed for, shrimp? It's not like gold will be of any use for a baby like you."

Nate screwed up his face. "I'm not a baby, I'm not! I could do plenty with gold."

"Oh, shut up," Rory said, poking his brother in the shoulder. "We don't have time for a temper tantrum."

Before Rory could retaliate again, Zach rose to his feet, placing his bolt cutters back into his backpack. "I'll bet it's darker than that," he said. "I bet it's a mass grave of all those people who've gone missing. I bet someone in this town, someone important like the sheriff, is a serial killer, and no one's brave enough to report it, so they just keep hiding his handiwork."

Nate blanched. He didn't want to see a dead body!

"Damn, dude," Beau said. "That's dark."

Zach shrugged. "Makes the most sense to me. That's why I brought a camera," he said, patting his backpack. "If that is what it is, I'm taking photos for proof so we can notify some reporter. We'll be famous for shining a light on something so heinous." He flashed a smug grin.

Rory grinned back and punched Zach lightly in the shoulder. "Good thinking, bro!"

Zach pulled aside the section of fence he'd cut loose and held it open for the others. Beau and Rory passed through without hesitation, but Nate hung back, chewing on his knuckles. "C'mon, squirt, are you coming or what?" Zach asked impatiently.

"I think we should go home," Nate said quietly. "I don't want to see any dead bodies."

Zach rolled his eyes. "Yo, Rory, deal with your little brother, will ya?" As Rory walked back up to the fence, he added, "I don't know why the heck you even brought him along."

Rory grimaced. "It's because of our story about the carnival. My mom said I had to take him there too. If I'd tried to fight it, she probably would've grounded me." He turned his attention to Nate. "We're not wasting anymore time, Nate. Either get a move on, or sit over there on that log and wait for us," he said, pointing at a fallen tree trunk. "Don't try to walk home by yourself 'cause you'll just get lost."

"But Rory…" Nate wailed. But when the boys turned and continued walking and it became apparent that they really wouldn't turn around, he hurried after them. He struggled through the fence opening, tearing his shirt on the sharp metal edges. "Wait for me, Rory, please!" Much to his relief, Rory did glance over his shoulder and slow his pace minutely to allow him to catch up at a jog. When he caught up, he grabbed the back of Rory's jacket and clutched the fabric in his fingers.

Rory looked down. "What're you doing?"

Nate just shook his head, eyes wide in fear. He was scared to death what they would find, and he had a really sick feeling in his gut.

Rory sighed, but he didn't shake Nate off. His little brother might be annoying, but he didn't hate him either. Let the kid hang on if it made him feel better and kept him quiet. The four boys walked through the trees a little farther until they reached a clearing. Rory stopped dead in his tracks. "What the…" he gasped, trailing off. Before them was a large hole with a crisscrossed metal grate over the top of it.

Nate sniffled next to him. "What is it? Is it a mine?"

Zach and Beau stood frozen nearby too, staring at the sight

before them. "No," Zach finally said. "That's not a mine." Slowly, he inched closer to the rim of the hole, Beau right on his heels. Rory followed suit, towing Nate along in his wake via his jacket.

They all came up to the rim of the hole and looked down. It was deep, or at least appeared deep with the sun at an angle. The pit was so dark they couldn't see the bottom. A vile stench wafted through the grate. "What the hell is that smell?" Beau asked. "Something rotting?"

Nate's heart pounded in his chest. Was it really a pit full of death bodies?

"No," Zach replied, frowning as he thought. "It' more like... like sickness. Or disease." He started walking along the perimeter of the pit, looking for any clues as to what it was.

Rory followed along, tugging Nate with him. "Rory," Nate said in a wobbly voice. "Rory, I want to go home now. Please!"

Rory swallowed thickly, eyes fixed on the pit. He put on a tough front, not wanting the others to see that he was getting freaked out too. "We'll go in a bit. We got all the way out here, we want to see what this is." He and Nate passed by Zach who'd stopped to peer down into the darkness again. Beau trailed along slowly behind all of them, seemingly even less interested in investigating.

"Woah," Rory breathed. He stared down at a gate in the grate. It had a latch like a backyard gate, but no lock, and he absentmindedly fiddled with it. It moved easily, and as the metal shrieked with the movement, he heard something even more frightening.

"What is it?" a sinister voice crooned from below. "Are there more?"

Rory startled back and flailed as he lost his balance. He bumped into Nate and watched in horror as everything seemed to slow down as his little brother landed on top of the gate. The latch that Rory had messed with earlier slipped free, and Nate was dumped into the darkness below. "Nate!" Rory screamed. He lunged forward, but he was far too late. Nate has vanished into the abyss.

Nate screamed as he plummeted, falling silent as air abandoned his lungs upon impact with the ground below. Slowly he sat up and looked all around. It was so dark down there! Up above he could see a small circle of light where his brother and his friends were. He could hear them screaming.

"I've gotta get him!" Rory was yelling.

"It's too late, man," Zach countered. There was the sound of scuffling. "Dude, he's gone. We have to get out of here! Beau, get the gate."

As Nate watched, a small shadow appeared in the light, and he heard the gate being pulled back in place. "No, don't leave me! Rory!" Nate clamped his mouth shut as he heard footsteps approaching next to him.

A match was struck and used to light a lantern, which someone then held high. Nate shrank back into the dirt wall of the pit behind him as the man with the lantern advanced closer and closer. The man held the lantern high enough for Nate to see the deranged smile on his face. He came so close and crouched down until his nose was nearly touching Nate's. The whites of his eyes were a dark red, so dark they were nearly black. The horrible smell from before seemed to ooze from him, and Nate felt the man's breath on his face as he spoke. "We all have it in here. We're all infected."

Nate sobbed and lunged to the side, dodging around the frightening man and running as fast as he could. He found that the pit exited into a tunnel, and he ran blindly down it. Here and there, small lights were placed to keep it from being nothing but absolute darkness, but it was dim. As he ran, Nate passed other people, all with gross eyes, all who turned unsettling grins towards him. Some greeted him and reached out for him as he ran by, others laughed at his fear. He didn't stop, afraid to even look at any of them, much less talk.

He turned down a smaller tunnel and saw a small amount of light above him. A ventilation shaft! The wall here was slightly sloped and soft. He dug his hands and feet into the earth and started struggling to climb up the steep grade.

"You can't go," a voice behind him said.

He looked over his shoulder and saw a young girl watching him. Though her eyes were as eerie as the rest, some part of his brain recognized her as the daughter of a family that had gone missing earlier in the year. He ignored her and doubled his efforts to climb out. He gave a wordless yell as he felt hands grab his leg and drag him back down.

"I said you can't leave!" the girl yelled at him, hands still gripping his leg. "You're one of us now."

"Let me go!" Nate shrieked, lashing out with a fist. He connected with her face, striking her as hard as he could. Her skin felt far too soft beneath his hand, and he saw it tear and split open from the force of his blow. She staggered back stunned, and instead of bleeding, her wound seemed to ooze a dark, rusty, viscous fluid.

Nate turned again and pulled himself up the wall as fast as he could. Below, he heard her screaming for help. By the time he made it to the top, he was wheezing, and he was afraid to look behind himself, both unwilling to see the distance below him and also afraid to see who may be following him. He looked at the grate above his head. It was the same as the one before, except this one had no gate. Nate's stomach seemed to plummet, but he dug furiously at the edge of the grate with his hands, hoping to be able to dislodge enough of the earth to squeeze through, grateful for the first time in his life that he was small for his age.

Outside, the sunny day was gone and dark rain clouds ruled the sky. Nate kept pawing at the earth as rain began pouring from the sky, loosening the earth for him. Finally, he felt his hand break through, and he redoubled his efforts. Slowly but surely he made a wide enough hole to get his arms and head through, and he squeezed his whole body through, collapsing on the ground once outside as he sobbed tears of exhausted relief. Still, he knew he couldn't risk staying there for long. Nate drew a deep breath to steady his nerves and heaved himself to his feet before trudging through the rain back to the tree line to try and find his way home.

The trek was long and dismal, and the rain only grew harder as daylight slowly faded away. Nate stumbled along, shoes squelching in the muddy earth, feeling entirely miserable. His chest shook periodically as he tried to suppress more tears, and his eyes burned and stung from all the tears and rain washing through them. But finally, he found himself emerging from the forest again and standing on a hill overlooking the town. Hope renewed, he hurried on down the sloping earth, passing surreptitiously around the other houses until he finally made it to his home. Through the windows he could hear his father's raised voice and his brother's timid replies and in the background his mother crying.

He let himself through the front door and immediately called for his mother. "Mom!"

"Nate?!" his mother shrieked. She burst into the room and

immediately scooped him into a hug, crying heavily as she clutched him close. "Oh, baby, I was so worried. Where were you?"

Nate's father also hurried into the room and crouched beside him, trying to peer around his mother's arms to check on his condition. "Son, are you okay? Are you hurt?"

Lingering at the edge of the room, Rory stood watching the reunion wide-eyed. One of his cheeks was bright red, like he'd probably been struck by one of their parents. He didn't come any closer, probably afraid of getting in trouble again, Nate thought. Or perhaps he was afraid of Nate?

Nate's mother asked again where he'd been, so this time he answered. "I fell into a hole."

"A hole?" his mother asked, confused. "Like a sink hole? Or an old mineshaft?"

"That doesn't matter, honey," Nate's father countered. "Give the boy some breathing room. If he fell, he could be injured. Nate, are you feeling any pain?"

Nate rubbed his eyes. "My eyes hurt. They're stinging."

"Here, let me see," said his mom. She released her hug and pried his eyes open gently, only to scream in terror, lurching away from him instinctively.

"Mommy?" Nate asked, hurt to feel so rejected after the horrible day he'd had.

She grabbed her husband. "His eyes! He...he has it..."

Nate's dad surveyed him with a horrified gaze before rounding on Rory and grabbing his upper arm. *"Where did you go today?"* he asked in a dangerous voice.

"Ow!" Rory cried, grabbing his arm where his dad squeezed it. "We...we went to the forbidden zone. Nate...he fell into the pit by accident."

"You did what?" cried their mother.

"What is wrong with you?" their father shouted.

"I don't understand," Nate sniffled, rubbing at his eyes again. "Are we in trouble?"

"The miners ran into something deep in the earth," their father growled, still staring down at Rory. "We don't know what it is, but it makes people sick. And it's very contagious, so we remove families from the town as soon as anyone contracts it. We've been quarantining them in an abandoned series of mines contained within that fence you foolishly passed beyond."

Nate reached out for his mother again and she shied away instinctively. Her face was stricken, clearly torn between desire to care for her frightened child and fear of what his eyes so clearly showed he carried.

"What?" Rory asked his father, dumbfounded. "How do more people not know about this?"

"The town elders wanted it kept quiet to keep a bunch of government suits from taking over. We're small enough that it wasn't difficult to ensure everyone's silence. Your mom and I chose to stay here because we don't work in the mine, so we figured we were safe. But you've just doomed us all," he added, finally releasing Rory's arm as he shoved him away in disgust.

"Do we have to go live with the people in the pit?" Nate asked in a small voice. His whole family looked at him in alarm. "They were scary; I want to stay here."

"No," his mother said. "No no no no no. Maybe there's some way...maybe we can hide this?" she asked her husband.

He started to reply, but before any words could come from his mouth, there was a thundering knock at their door.

Unkempt Hair

Stacy stood before her bathroom mirror, tongue sticking out between her lips as she concentrated on what she was doing. Ever so carefully, she worked on the complicated plait she wanted to wear today. She'd watched a tutorial video online and then spent a large amount of her free time over the weekend practicing it so that come Monday morning, she'd be able to perfect it before she had to leave for school. Finally, the last pin in place, she raised a handheld mirror to admire her hair from all sides. She grinned, proud of herself for the intricate series of braids wrapped around her head like something out of a fantasy movie. She looked like an elven queen, and she knew she would garner a lot of attention from her friends at school, and with any luck, from Tommy Fischer too. It was the perfect debut for the first day of her senior year.

With a final grin at her reflection, she put away her mirror and slipped back into her room to grab her backpack, hastily stuffing her belongs into the bag last minute. Then she jogged down the stairs to join her parents for breakfast before they all set out for their days. A selection of cereals was set out on the table along with the milk. Her mother sat at the table reading the paper while sipping her coffee, and her father lingered over by the counter, waiting like a hawk for his toast to pop up from the toaster. "Morning, honey," he said as she entered the room. "Toast?" he asked.

"No, thanks!" she replied, grabbing the box of Raisin Bran. As she poured cereal into her bowl, she glanced at her mom. "Anything interesting in there today?" she asked.

Her mom sighed and folded the paper aside. "Nope, just the usual doom and gloom." She smiled tiredly, but then perked up. "Oh, but there *is* going to be some excitement for us!"

Stacy raised her eyebrows. Their lifestyle certainly wasn't anything to scoff at, but it also wasn't what anyone could consider exciting. "Well spill the beans, then," she said, nudging her mom's foot with hers.

"Mrs. Briggs, the guidance counselor from your school, called us this morning." Stacy nodded, vaguely aware of having heard the phone ring while she was getting ready. "Your school is getting a set of foreign exchange students this semester, and it seems Mr. And Mrs. Simmons—you know, from around the block—were planning to host one of them, but Mrs. Simmons, the poor dear, broke her hip last night when she fell from a ladder." Her mother shook her head. "She's scheduled for surgery today to repair the damage, but it'll be a long recovery, and her husband will have his hands full caring for her, so they really aren't in any position to host now. Their charge—a young girl from China named Mingmei—is already here, but Mrs. Briggs is in a frenzy trying to find someone who is able to host an exchange student on such short notice."

Stacy's mouth fell open. "And that's going to be us?" She felt an odd mix of excitement and hesitation. On the one hand, it would be cool to have someone new to meet and someone her own age in the home rather than it aways just being her and her parents, but on the other hand, what if the girl didn't like her? What if they didn't get along? And, selfish as it seemed, this was her senior year. It was supposed to be about her transition into adulthood, and just the mention of this new girl almost felt like her thunder was being stolen. Still, she shoved all of those thoughts aside. The poor girl needed somewhere to stay; it surely couldn't be easy for her to have all her plans blown up in smoke thanks to a freak accident. She knew should be more charitable.

"Yep!" her dad said, sitting at the table with his heap of four pieces of toast. "After the sign-up deadline to be a host passed by at the end of last semester, your mom and I regretted not considering it more. We thought it would be good for you to have exposure to someone from another culture. And now that all of this has happened, we figure this is fate's strange way of providing us with a second chance."

Her mom stood up to take her breakfast dishes to the counter. "Mrs. Briggs is taking care of getting Mingmei to school this morning, and then your father and I will come and pick you both up from school this afternoon."

Stacy felt herself deflate a little. "Oh, but…I had plans to go to out with Kay and Minda after school today."

Stacy's mother waved her hand dismissively. "You'll have plenty of time to hang out with them this school year. This is Mingmei's first day at an American school and only her second week in America. The least we can do is all be there for her and welcome her as a family.

Stacy wanted to protest; Kay had been out of town visiting family for the second half of the summer, and she and Minda had both put in a lot of hours working summer jobs, so they hadn't seen each other much either. But she knew her mother well and knew when an argument was already lost before it began, so she swallowed her complaints. "Fine," she said, getting up and pouring the milk from her cereal down the drain.

Her mother was already out the door and into the garage. "Hurry up, Stacy! We need to get going if I'm going to have enough time to get you to school before work."

Stacy turned to pick up her bag, and her dad stopped her with a tap on her arm. "Huh?" she said.

He smiled. "Your hair looks very lovely today."

She felt herself break into a grin, pleased that at least one of them had noticed. "Thanks, Dad!" she said, grabbing him in a one-armed hug before hurrying for the garage.

~~~

The school day was a whirlwind of reunions and getting back into the swing of things. Stacy was in several advanced classes, and by the end of the day, she was already weary of the emphasis every teacher was putting on the importance of this last year in preparation for college. More than anything, she really just wanted to go unwind with her friends, but instead of heading with them to the student parking lot out back, she made her way to the front of the building where her parents would be picking her up. She hadn't met her new house mate yet—because she was a junior, they didn't share any classes—but she'd heard a few comments flittering around in the halls about a standout new student and wondered if it might be Mingmei.

When she made it outside and saw her parents' car in the distance, the two of them standing outside with Mrs. Briggs and a young girl, she decided her assumptions must have been right. This must be the girl everyone was talking about. She wasn't very tall, but she had a stunning length of shining black hair that, while wild and untamed, was still gorgeous. It cascaded down her back to her thighs and curled over her shoulders, along her neck and down her front, framing a face with a creamy complexion and striking dark eyes.

"Ah, Stacy!" her mom said, waving her over. "You've finally made it. Mingmei was just telling us she hadn't had a chance to meet you yet. Mingmei, this is our daughter, Stacy."

Mingmei cocked her head, raised her hand in a wave, and smiled sweetly. "Hi! It's good to meet you. I am so excited to have a sister!"

Stacy smiled and waved in return, but for some reason that she couldn't quite put her finger on, she felt uncomfortable. "It's good to meet you too. It'll be fun to have someone other than just mom and dad around this year." She nudged her father in the arm as she spoke so that they would know she meant it as a joke, not an insult.

Mrs. Briggs smiled big. "Yes, little Mingmei here specifically said she was hoping for a family with a girl close to her age, which is why I thought of you all first." Her smile faded a little. "I'm just so glad that we were able to tidy up this unfortunate turn of events so quickly and find a home for Mingmei. I still can't believe how Mrs. Simmons ended up hurting herself. She's a little advanced in years, but she and her husband worked house renovation together for years, so she's been up and down ladders forever."

Stacy's father nodded sympathetically. "Just a freak accident, I suppose," he replied. "But we're certainly happy to step in and help out."

Mrs. Briggs nodded, then glanced at her watch. "Well, I'll have to leave you to it now. I have quite a bit more to do today before I can go home."

They exchanged farewells, and Stacy, her family, and Mingmei all headed for home. The entire car ride home, her parents made easy conversation, asking Mingmei all kinds of things about her interests and how life and school seemed different between her home in China and there in the United States. Stacy stayed quiet for the most part, only speaking if directly spoken to, trying to put her finger on what was causing the unsettling feeling she had while sitting in the backseat next to Mingmei. She looked at her out of the corner of her eye. Mingmei sat very prim and proper, hardly taking up any space except for her wave of hair pooling all along the back of the seat and into the space between the two of them. Stacy shook her head and scooted slightly from it. She really should do something to control it, she thought.

~~~

The week continued on, and all Stacy seemed to hear about was Mingmei. How great she was, how pretty, how smart. Kids at school, teachers at school, her parents—everyone seemed to just adore her. By the end of the first week, Stacy was already sick of it. She tried to be reasonable about it; Mingmei was new and from another country and yes, pretty, so it made sense that she'd immediately been so popular. But it felt like such an intrusion, and no matter how hard she tried, Stacy couldn't seem to feel the same about her as everyone else did.

All the same, there was nothing she could do about it. Mingmei moved into the room across the hall from Stacy's that connected through a shared bathroom between the rooms. It was the bathroom that became the epitome of Mingmei's intrusion on Stacy's life. She left her mark on it every day by little bits of hair on the floor and in the shower. Every day without fail, long strands of dark hair collecting over everything. Every day Stacy cleared it up with distaste, but it made no difference. She wanted to say something, but didn't know how she was supposed to do that without making it awkward and without getting her mother on her case for being a rude host.

On top of the dislike that she couldn't shake, Stacy was also plagued by an uncomfortable feeling, like there was something wrong about Mingmei. But Mingmei was soft spoken and pleasant, and Stacy knew there wasn't any good explanation for her feelings. She knew no one would see things the way she did, so she decided to keep her feelings to herself and try to avoid Mingmei as much as possible. With a little effort, she'd be able to make everything work out.

~~~

When Friday came, Stacy was invited to a party at Minda's boyfriend's home. "A little bird told me that Tommy would be there," Minda said with a knowing gaze. "Think you might be interested in coming?"

Stacy grinned in response and couldn't help the blush that crossed her face. "Definitely! I'll see you at 7:00!"

After school, when Stacy told her mom and dad that she would be going out, they had no issue with her plans, as expected. What was not expected, though, was their insistence that she take Mingmei along with her.

"What?" Stacy asked. "But it's not my party to just bring other guests to, Mom. I was invited."

Her mom waved her hand dismissively. "Nonsense, Stacy.

Mingmei is new here and is living with us. Your friends shouldn't have any problem with you bringing her along." Then she looked at Stacy sharply. "And don't think I haven't noticed you distancing yourself from her. I don't know what your issue is, but you need to straighten up and be more welcoming. She's new here and all alone; she needs friends."

Stacy struggled to find a way to say that Mingmei seemed to be finding friends perfectly fine and didn't need her as one too, but it was too late. Mingmei came down from her room where she'd disappeared right after school, and Stacy's mom charged right in and told her about the party. "You should go! It'll be a great way to meet new people!"

Mingmei's eyes lit up and she smiled big. "Oh, that sounds fun! It's okay if I come with you?" she asked, turning to Stacy.

Stacy knew she took a beat too long getting her face to an amicable expression, but she didn't care. "Yeah, of course. I'm leaving at 6:45."

"Great!" Mingmei said with a clap of her hands, either not noticing or not acknowledging Stacy's obvious reluctance. "I'll get ready." She turned in a whirl of hair and rushed back to her room.

"See, look how excited she is," Stacy's mom said. "And to think you weren't even going to invite her. Honestly, Stacy, I'm disappointed in you." And then she walked away, leaving Stacy feeling dejected and alone in the middle of the kitchen.

The uneasy feeling prickled at the back of her neck again. She had been looking forward to a night of her own with her friends, and again Mingmei was getting in the middle of it. As she headed for her room, Stacy had to concede that it really wasn't Mingmei's fault, it was her mom's, but still….

When she got back to her room, she opened the door to the

bathroom only to find Mingmei leaning over the sink to get closer to the mirror as she applied some makeup. "Oh, sorry," Stacy mumbled, starting to close the door.

"It's okay. You can get ready too," Mingmei said with a wave.

"No, it's fine. I'll work on picking my outfit for now, and I'll wait until you're done with the bathroom." Stacy wasn't in the mood to be stuck in such a confined space with Mingmei. Even more annoyed now, she turned for her closet instead to put together an outfit that would be sure to impress Tommy Fischer and catch his eye.

~~~

Some time later, they were finally in Stacy's car, nearly at the party. Stacy's mood had not improved. After she'd finally gotten possession of the bathroom, she'd found hair *everywhere*, much more than she ever had before. On the counter, on the toilet lid, all over the floor. It was like Mingmei had gone mad with a brush and spun like a twister while working with it. Stacy once again had cleaned it all up, first brushing pieces from the counter into the trash can, and then collecting the large amount from the floor to also add to the trash, grimacing in disgust as the hair almost seemed to cling to her fingers, unwilling to release her. She just couldn't wrap her head around how Mingmei would even begin to think that leaving hair everywhere was okay. She couldn't help but wonder if it was intentional.

And it wasn't even like whatever she'd done to her hair had done much good, Stacy thought, sending an annoyed glance at Mingmei in the passenger's seat. Her hair was still just as large and wild as ever, seeming to billow around her like a cloud.

Stacy couldn't believe that she wouldn't at least pull some of it back or braid it or something to rein it in. She herself had chosen a simple yet elegant French braid to tidy up her hair.

When they arrived at the party location, they found that many of the people were outside in the enormous backyard enjoying one of the last warm nights of summer before autumn completely took over on its prelude to winter. After scanning the backyard crowd, Stacy headed into the house to look for Kay and Minda, only halfway noticing that Mingmei didn't stay with her. Stacy hugged her friends when she found them and immediately told them about having had to bring Mingmei along. She kept the rest to herself, not wanting to be a gossip; she just needed to vent her frustrations that her mom seemed intent on pushing Mingmei into every aspect of her life.

Kay and Minda were appropriately sympathetic, having heard from Stacy already about her dislike for Mingmei. But then finally, Minda, with a cheeky grin, said, "I know what'll make you feel better. Let's go and find Tommy. You look so *hot* tonight. I just know if you bat those eyes at him, he'll finally ask you out!"

Stacy giggled and let her friends drag her back outside to go and find Tommy. "Ah ha!" exclaimed Kay. "There he is. Uh…oh no…."

Kay tried to pull Stacy back, but not before Stacy saw it. Tommy was sitting on a picnic table bench, and next to him, practically sitting in his lap, was Mingmei. He has his arm around her, and she leaned into him, her stupid hair draped all around him. As Stacy watched, Tommy said something, and Mingmei laughed, nuzzling her face into his. And just for a moment, her eyes flashed up to Stacy's and she smirked triumphantly. And then the moment passed, and she was back to being an adorable little girl giggling at Tommy's every word and pulling him in for a kiss.

Stacy turned on her heel and stormed back into the house, feeling angry tears prickling at her eyes. She'd spent all summer dreaming of dating Tommy, and it was all over. She sat down in the least crowded corner of the living room, and Kay and Minda hurried after her, trying their best to console her, but she shook her head. "She did this on purpose," she growled.

"On purpose?" Kay asked. "Why would she do that? Did you tell her that you liked Tommy?"

"No," Stacy replied. "I've never talked to her about him. No one but you two knows that I like him." She saw the two of them exchange a skeptical gaze. "Look, I know it sounds crazy, but it's not. Just now she…she looked at me and.…" She trailed off as they looked at her with pity more than anything. "Just forget it." She stood up and straightened her shoulders. "I don't feel much like partying anymore. I'm going."

"Oh, Stacy, don't be that way," Minda whined. "You should stay." When Stacy shook her head and headed for the front door, Minda asked, "What about Mingmei? Do you want one of us to bring her home later?"

Stacy gritted her teeth. She was so angry, she wanted nothing more than to just leave right now and let Mingmei find her own way home. But she knew without a doubt that her mother would be furious with her for doing that. She let out a defeated sigh. "No, I'll drive her home. I'm just going to go wait in my car." And without a backward glance, she marched out of the house to go sulk in her car alone.

~~~

It was a couple of hours before Mingmei finally joined Stacy in her car to go home. "Oh my," she said as she slid into the passenger seat, "have you been waiting long?"

Stacy eyed her, trying to figure her out. Gone was the snide smirk from earlier, and in its place that cutesy demeanor she used with everyone else. "I just didn't feel much like partying after all," she finally said coldly, turning the car on as she did.

Mingmei widened her eyes in apparent sympathy. "You should have found me! We could have left earlier. I did not know you wanted to leave."

Stacy bit her tongue to keep from snapping back. She knew what she'd seen, knew that Mingmei had seen her and gloated over the fact that she had scored a place beside Tommy instead of her. But she didn't know *how* she'd known about her interest in Tommy, and she couldn't prove it. Yet. But that niggling feeling that was like an itch between her shoulder blades was stronger than ever, warning her that Mingmei was a threat. "It's fine," she said, finally forcing a fake smile. "I knew you were excited to party, so I was fine with waiting."

They paused at a stop sign, and Stacy looked over just in time to see Mingmei run her hand through her hair, letting the long strands flow through her fingers. Mingmei smiled again, the sweetness absent this time. "Thank you. I had a lot of fun. Especially with Tommy." She smirked a little and her eyes were dark. Then it all faded again, and she glanced at her watch. "You should hurry. Your mom might worry."

Stacy didn't hide her own dark look in response. But instead just said in a measured tone, "Yeah, we should make sure not to worry her."

When they got home, Stacy got out of having to sit around telling her mom about the party alongside Mingmei by feigning a headache. She went into the bathroom, washed off all her makeup and let her hair loose from her braid, and then changed into her pajamas, flopping onto her bed dejectedly. She reached down to open her nightstand drawer and pulled out her journal. She knew she was too wound up to fall asleep right away and wanted to write down all of her feelings from tonight. There were pages and pages devoted to her crush on Tommy, so it was only fitting that she update the journal with tonight's setback. She'd also been writing in it lately about Mingmei, recording her reticence about the new girl. Two birds with one stone today, she thought bitterly. But when she opened the journal, she had to bite back a scream. There, between the pages where she'd last written, was a thick, twisted clump of long black hair.

~~~

Stacy set an alarm for early the following morning. She knew her mom would be going into the office this Saturday, so she would be up early to get herself a little breakfast before leaving. Stacy wanted to be sure she could talk to her alone. She didn't know what exactly to say or how to make her case, but she had decided she was right to feel uncomfortable around Mingmei. She didn't know what her deal was, if she was just weird, or a sociopath, or what, but there was something wrong, and she needed to make her mom understand. When the alarm went off, she hurried downstairs, and as expected, her mom was at the table.

"Good morning, Stacy," her mom said, glancing up from the paper as she entered the room. "You're up early for a Saturday."

Stacy slid into a seat at the table. "Yeah, I wanted to have a chance to talk to you before you went to work today."

Stacy's mom raised her eyebrows. "Okay." She folded the paper and set it aside, then took a sip of her coffee. "What do you want to talk about?"

After taking a deep breath, Stacy replied, "It's about Mingmei." Her mom's face didn't change from the flat expression she'd put on as soon as their conversation began. "She's...Mom, she's really weird. There's something not right about her. She's always leaving hair all over the bathroom, and then at the party last night, she went straight for Tommy Fischer because she knew I liked him and—"

Her mom cut her off with a raise of her hand. "So she's weird because she sheds hair like a normal human being and because she was lucky enough to attract the attention of a boy that you weren't?"

Stacy gaped at her. "I'm not jealous that Tommy liked her, I'm saying she only tried to get him to spite me! She gave me a look last night when she was practically laying all over him. She's putting on a facade. She's always acting so cute and sweet around everyone, but she's been really snide towards me."

Stacy's mom stood and carried her coffee mug over to the sink. "Well it's no wonder she's not as polite to you as she is to others, Stacy. People respond to the treatment they are given, and you haven't been welcoming at all. She told me about how you abandoned her at the party last night and she was all on her own to meet new people. She's lucky that that nice boy, Tommy, was kind enough to take care of her."

"What? That's not...." Stacy realized with a sinking feeling the mistake she'd made the night before by going straight to bed.

"Your attitude has really become a problem this year, Stacy," her mom said. "I'd had high hopes that you'd finish your senior year strong and be ready to start a successful college career, but this poor disposition of yours is only going to cause you problems in the long run. I suggest a good long look in the mirror before it's too late." She collected her purse and headed for the garage.

"Wait. Mom, you're not listening to me. I found her hair in my *journal.* There's something *wrong* with her. *Mom*!" But it was too late. Her mother had brushed her aside, and through the door, Stacy could hear the garage door opening and the car starting. It was no use. Mingmei had her mom under her thumb just like everyone else, and her dad was probably the same. She already knew her friends thought she was just jealous, and even if they did side with her, they really couldn't help that much. There had to be *somebody* she could go to.

Stacy recalled Mingmei's first day with the family when her parents arrived to collect her from the school. Mrs. Briggs had said how surprising it was that Mrs. Simmons, the original host mom, had fallen from a ladder when she was so experienced with them. She chewed on her lip. Something wasn't right there either. And come to think of it, Mrs. Simmons and her husband had never called to check in on how Mingmei was doing in her new home. Sure, they would be caught up in Mrs. Simmons' recovery, but under normal circumstances, one would think they'd show concern or interest in the girl they were planning to care for during an entire school semester. Stacy turned decisively and went upstairs to get dressed. She was going to go and talk to Mrs. Simmons.

~~~

A while later, Stacy found herself awkwardly standing before the Simmons' house, trying to decide how she was going to ask the questions she had. A figure on the screened-in porch waved at her, startling her from her thoughts. It was Mrs. Simmons. She was reclined back on a comfy looking chair. Stacy waved back and approached, letting herself onto the porch. "Good morning, Mrs. Simmons," she said, taking a seat next to her. "How are you feeling?"

Mrs. Simmons smiling, creasing the wrinkles on her face more sharply. "I'm doing just fine, dear. Thank you. My husband just finished getting me settled out here. The weather is so nice, I wanted to be able to sit out here and enjoy it."

"That sounds lovely, Mrs. Simmons," Stacy replied. "I'm glad you have such a nice space to enjoy the weather without having to sit in the sun all day." She trailed off, trying to figure out how to proceed.

"What's on your mind, dear?" Mrs. Simmons asked. "I appreciate you coming by to see how I'm feeling, but I suspect you have something more on your mind to come all the way over here on a Saturday morning."

Stacy bit her lip. "You're right. Um…I wanted to ask you about your accident. Everyone was saying how uncharacteristic it was for you to fall from a ladder. What happened?"

Mrs. Simmons sighed. "I really don't know," she said quietly. "It doesn't make any sense to me either. I was on my way down, and it was like…well it was almost as though my foot got caught up with some kind of string, like a wire stretched across the ladder. And so I got off balance and I fell."

Stacy chewed on a fingernail. "A string, huh. Or maybe hair?" She wasn't really speaking to Mrs. Simmons, but she saw her fix her with a sharp gaze at her comment. They stared at each other a moment, almost like they shared an idea but were both too afraid to voice it aloud. To break the awkward silence, Stacy asked, "What was Mingmei like for that first week she lived with you?"

There was no mistake; Mrs. Simmons face visibly paled slightly at the mention of her name. "Oh, she was…fine. A very quiet girl, kept mostly to herself. She was upset when she found out that our daughter was grown and didn't live in the house anymore. Apparently she was really looking forward to living with someone her own age. My husband and I have enjoyed hosting foreign exchange students during the years that your school invites them because we miss having our daughter at home, but this year…well, we didn't really get to do it long this year…but this year wasn't really the same."

Stacy hesitated a moment, then decided to be honest. "Mingmei is living with my parents and me now, and she really makes me uncomfortable. There's just something weird about her." She watched Mrs. Simmons closely and could tell that she was thinking. But when she spoke, it wasn't what she wanted to hear.

"Yes, sometimes it's the difference in culture that makes it hard to get along at first. But I'm sure it'll all be fine." Her face was expressionless, as though whatever she'd thought or felt earlier had been push somewhere deep down.

Stacy sighed. "Yeah, maybe." She stood to go. "Thank you, Mrs. Briggs. I hope your recovery goes quickly." As she was making her way through the door, Mrs. Brigg's voice made her pause.

"You look out for yourself this semester, dear. Please be careful."

Stacy absorbed the solemn look on Mrs. Simmons' face, and she understood. Mrs. Simmons felt the same as she did and "knew" what she knew. But she wouldn't say any more than that. Because how could they? No one would believe that there could be anything sinister about a sweet, young exchange student named Mingmei.

~~~

Stacy already felt exhausted when she got back home, and it wasn't even quite midday. When she walked through the door, she planned on heading back to her room to do some more thinking, but instead she found Mingmei sitting in the living room, almost as though she were waiting for her. "Where's my dad?" Stacy asked, immediately on alert.

Mingmei smiled, but no longer was it even remotely sweet. It was crooked and cruel, and her eyes contained only malice. "He's not here," she replied calmly, her voice distinctly colder than it ever had been before. "He went to the store." She looked up at Stacy. "Now we finally have some time alone, just the two of us. I have so been looking forward to this."

Every instinct in Stacy told her to run. She pivoted and grabbed the front door handle, but it wouldn't turn. She looked down and found that hair had been wrapped all around it, sticking it tight. She let go as if burned by it, then looked all around. She could see through to the kitchen, and even from a distance could see the harsh black hair against the background of white paint on the door, holding that doorknob fast too. She returned her gaze to Mingmei and found that she was now standing, eyes still fixed raptly on Stacy like a predator's on prey. "What are you?" she asked.

Mingmei stroked the hair that fell over her shoulder serenely, and the hair seemed to move on its own. As Stacy watched, the hair atop her head moved until it raised up, revealing tendrils like tiny legs that seemed almost sewn down into her head. "The girl is a vessel, a spent one," said an inhuman voice, but not through Mingmei's mouth; her eyes had gone flat and glassy as the hair arose. "You might call me a monster or a demon."

Stacy stared transfixed at the impossible sight before her. "What do you want?" she finally managed to ask.

An eerie chuckle seemed to echo around the room. "You."

Stacy turned and ran, racing up the stairs, desperate to get to the bathroom. A feral shriek behind her fueled her speed, and she made it to the bathroom, ripping a drawer open to find what she sought. Hair cutting scissors. Just as her hand clasped over them, hair wrapped around her other arm and her legs, pulling her back. Stacy screamed and lashed out viciously with the scissors, cutting every scrap of hair she could reach. The tendrils let her go with a cry of pain, and she ran again back downstairs, planning to use the scissors to get the hair off the doorknob and escape.

She tripped over something at the bottom of the stairs and screamed when she realized it was the lifeless body of Mingmei, hairless and rapidly degrading before her eyes. At the top of the stairs the hair almost seemed to float, supporting itself with tendrils attached here and there to light fixtures and the banister.

"Clever young girl," the evil voice rumbled, "but you will not escape me."

Tears prickled the corners of Stacy's eyes. She stood and backed away, the hand with the scissors extended, shaking, before her. "Stay away from me," she said feebly. "Leave me alone."

The hair slowly followed, releasing and extending tendrils

to move itself along the banister, it's motion like a spider. "It's your own fault," it said. "I was going to wait longer and decide whether I wanted you, the convenient prey, or someone else, but you're too perceptive for your own good. I have no choice now; I must keep you quiet."

Stacy shook her head. "No, I won't say anything, I swear. Please, just leave me alone!" Her voice arced into a scream as the hair suddenly rushed forward, multiple tendrils grasping for her. She raised her hands futilely, but the scissors were flung away from her. She fell to the ground and tried to fight the tendrils encircling her wrists, but in mere seconds, the main body of the hair was on her head, and the tendrils forced themselves into her scalp. As they wound through the top of her head, what had once been Stacy passed into oblivion.

~~~

A young girl stood getting ready for school, smiling in the mirror as she brushed out her beautiful, long black hair. It was long, large, and wild, and she loved it. She looked disdainfully at the collection of pins, barrettes, hair ties, and the like in the drawer before her, and she dumped them all into the trash can. She went down and had breakfast with her parents, and she went to school. For a split second, people wondered if she'd always had long black hair, but the thought was gone as soon as it was formed. Silly. Of course she had. Some teachers paused for a moment during roll call; hadn't there been one more student? No, of course not, the student roster was correct. When the girl kissed him in front of all of his friends, Tommy was almost taken aback, but then he grinned, running his hand through her beautiful hair and kissed her again.

On the way home, the girl passed by a lovely house with a lovely screened-in patio on the front. An older woman sat in a large, cushioned chair. The girl stopped before the house and stood staring. The older woman saw her, and a look of deep horror overtook her features. The girl grinned and waved. "So good to see you're feeling well today!" she called. The woman didn't reply, only covered her mouth with her hand, eyes wide as could be. The woman wasn't a problem. She understood the reality of things, but more importantly, she knew the consequences if she didn't keep her mouth shut.

The girl continued on her way home, a satisfied smirk on her face. A fresh life was oh so deliciously good.

· T. M. DELANEY ·

About the Author

T. M. Delaney is a writer of novels and short stories. They live in Missouri with their cat Remy, their official creative "mews." T. M. Delaney spent several years working in publishing before changing to a career in graphic design. In their spare time, they love listening to music, reading, playing video games, and spending time with friends and family.

T. M. Delaney most commonly writes m/m romance novels, but also has plans for non-romance titles as well. Their interests are wide, including urban fantasy, magical realism, paranormal, and realistic fiction to name a few. Angst and comfort are their specialties, as is mixing spicy heat with tender sweetness.

Want to connect with this author? Check out their author newsletter at tmdelaney.substack.com for regular updates about their life, their writing projects, upcoming titles, and adorable pictures of their cat.

Subscribe to my newsletter:
✉ https://tmdelaney.substack.com

Also by T. M. Delaney

Eerie 2: A Collection of 10 Chilling Tales
A collection of 10 chilling tales of horror. What would you do if you woke up in the middle of nowhere with no memory? What if the grownups won't listen or care? What if you found out your whole life was a lie? What fate might await a door-to-door salesman with nefarious intent? Or a thief unwittingly targeting the wrong treasure? Delve into these tales if you dare.

Get your copy today: **books2read.com/Eerie-2-A-Collection-of-10-Chilling-Tales**

www.ingramcontent.com/pod-product-compliance
Lightning Source LLC
LaVergne TN
LVHW092054060526
838201LV00047B/1393